Fairies

The *Myths, Legends, & Lore*

S KYE A LEXANDER

Adams Media
New York London Toronto Sydney New Delhi

Adams Media
An Imprint of Simon & Schuster, Inc.
100 Technology Center Drive
Stoughton, MA 02072

For information about special discounts for bulk purchases, please contact Simon & Schuster Special Sales at 1-866-506-1949 or business@simonandschuster.com.

The Simon & Schuster Speakers Bureau can bring authors to your live event. For more information or to book an event contact the Simon & Schuster Speakers Bureau at 1-866-248-3049 or visit our website at www.simonspeakers.com.

Interior art © Dover Publications, Juniperimages Corporation, and 123rf.com.

Manufactured in the United States of America

13 2023

Library of Congress Cataloging-in-Publication Data has been applied for.

ISBN 978-1-4405-7305-7
ISBN 978-1-4405-7306-4 (ebook)

DEDICATION

In memory of Robert Norris, fellow writer and friend,

who loved life and lived it fully.

ACKNOWLEDGMENTS

I wish to thank my editor Peter Archer and all the creative spirits at Adams Media for giving me the opportunity to write this book. Heartfelt thanks also go to my friend Claire Tomlinson, who provided a magical retreat where I could hide out and write both *Fairies: The Myths, Legends, & Lore* and my previous book, *Mermaids: The Myths, Legends, & Lore*. I'm indebted, too, to the countless folklorists and fairy tale enthusiasts who have spent so many years collecting stories about fairies and making them available for the rest of us to enjoy.

Contents

Fascinating Fairies

"Of all the minor creatures of mythology, fairies are the most
beautiful, the most numerous, the most memorable."

 —Andrew Lang

The ancient Greeks called them nymphs. The Irish called them the little people. The Persians called them peris. Wherever you go on this planet you'll hear fairy tales of magical and mysterious beings, some no bigger than your hand and some taller than the redwoods. They fly through the air, tunnel deep into the earth, splash about in the seas, even flicker in candle flames. These awesome creatures have played a prominent role in the lives and legends of mortals since the beginning of time, and they still do.

In recent years, it seems as if fairies are everywhere. We're inundated with big-budget films, TV shows, and enough merchandise to fill every palace in fairyland—all devoted to fanciful beings who may or may not actually exist. What is it about fairies that keeps us in their thrall?

Like mermaids and dragons, fairies intrigue us because they're so complex. Some are bewitchingly beautiful, others are ugly enough to shatter mirrors—and just to keep us confused, they can change the way they look to appear however they want to be seen. Capricious characters, fairies embody good and evil, innocence and passion, playfulness and treachery—the juxtaposition of opposites is part of their appeal. We just never know what to expect from them, or what they'll do next. Will the fey give us pots of gold or turn us into toads? The risk entices us, as a flame entices moths. We also envy their freedom and power. Fairies don't have to abide by the rules of mortals; they can come and go as they please—even disappear entirely whenever they want. They possess an arsenal of magical abilities that enable them to overcome obstacles, enjoy wealth and longevity, and amuse themselves at the expense of humans. And if they really want to show who's boss, they can conjure up a hurricane or an earthquake faster than we can send a text. Of course, we also have them to thank for rainbows, flowers, and the changing leaves in autumn. Think how much duller the earth would be without the fairies!

Another reason we love fairies is because they take us out of our ordinary, everyday existence and whisk us away to fantastic places where anything can happen—and does. In the process, they show us different ways to view the world and what else can befall us in it. Furthermore, they challenge us to discover our own magic and to use our powers creatively.

In this book, you'll meet all sorts of fairies from around the world, including some who will surely surprise you. You'll also hear tales from people who've had close encounters with pixies, elves, or other spirits. Plus you'll learn ways to attract fairy companions—or get them to stop playing tricks on you. As you revisit the fairy tales and legends included here, you'll not only gain insights into the fey, but into yourself as well. You might even find you have a bit of fairy blood flowing in your veins.

PART ONE

The Fairy Realm

"[The children] made wreaths of flowers and hung them upon the tree and about the spring to please the fairies that lived there; for they liked that, being idle innocent little creatures, as all fairies are, and fond of anything delicate and pretty like wild flowers put together that way. And in return for this attention the fairies did any friendly thing they could for the children, such as keeping the spring always full and clear and cold, and driving away serpents and insects that sting; and so there was never any unkindness between the fairies and the children during more than five hundred years."

—Mark Twain, *Joan of Arc*

"If we opened our minds to enjoyment, we might find tranquil pleasures spread about us on every side. We might live with the angels that visit us on every sunbeam, and sit with the fairies who wait on every flower."

—Samuel Smiles

CHAPTER 1

Meet the Fairies

agical, mysterious, and mischievous, fairies never fail to enchant us. But what are they really? Most people consider fairies the products of human imagination—cartoon characters in animated movies or charming creatures in stories we read to children at bedtime—and unless you're under the age of six, you probably don't believe they exist. Or, if you're into fantasy games, you might think of fairies as personae you can assume in order to engage in mock battles with other pseudo-fairies. But if you delve a little deeper, you'll discover that all sorts of fanciful folk have populated the fairy world for thousands of years—and they're as diverse as the animal species who inhabit our planet. In this book we'll speak of them generically as "fairies," but these wondrous beings go by lots of different names: elves, pixies, dwarfs, and leprechauns, to name just a few. Let's meet some of them now.

A Fairy by Any Other Name

Back in the days when life was much more mysterious and people believed in an enchanted world, mortals feared offending the fairies who might cast spells or inflict curses on a whim. Calling a powerful supernatural being by its real name was considered disrespectful, so humans referred to fairies in euphemistic terms such as the Good People, the Gentry, the Shining Ones, and the Neighbors.

The English word "fairy" (or faery) may have come from the Latin *fatum*, meaning fate, as did the French derivative *fée*, the Italian *fata*, and the Spanish *fada*. Middle English used the term *faierie* (*faeire* in Old French) to refer to the land of enchantment and its inhabitants; today we call it Faerie. Of course, each culture not only had its own names for fairies, it also recognized various types of fairies—many of whom you'll meet in the following chapters. Certain of these fascinating beings, however, show up in the myths and lore of numerous countries, suggesting that either some fairy species reside in lots of different places or that as people migrated they brought tales of fairies with them—perhaps both.

Although flying fairies dominate the scene today, they didn't really become popular until the Victorian era. Instead, early legends in Europe, Britain, and Ireland tended to focus on the following fairy folk, whom we'll discuss more in Chapter 2.

- Pixies
- Elves
- Dwarfs
- Trolls
- Hags
- Leprechauns
- Goblins
- The Sidhe

Moyra Doorly, author of *No Place for God* and *The Council in Question*, dislikes the term "fairy" because it connotes the whimsical, "saccharine-coated" characters that decorate little girls' lunchboxes and T-shirts. She prefers to call these magical beings nature spirits "because in all my encounters with them I saw nothing resembling Tinkerbell."

Elementals

When magicians talk about the elements, they don't mean the periodic table you learned about in school. They're referring to the four elements—air, earth, water, and fire—that make up the natural world and beyond. Since ancient times, myths and legends have spoken about supernatural beings who fly through the air, burrow beneath the earth, or swim in the ocean's depths. But these magical creatures don't simply reside in these regions; they serve as guardians and ambassadors of their respective realms. Some people might describe them as energetic forces rather than specific entities, and they go by different names in different mystical traditions. In Eastern mysticism, divine beings known as devas (similar to angels or minor deities) direct the nature spirits. In the fairy world, the three most popular elementals are known as sylphs, sprites, and water nymphs. Fire fairies called salamanders also show up from time to time, but they're less prevalent.

"The function of the nature spirits of woodland, meadow, and garden . . . is to furnish the vital connecting link between the stimulating energy of the sun and the raw material of the form. That growth of a plant which we regard as the customary and inevitable result of associating the three factors of sun, seed, and soil would never take place if the fairy builders were absent."

—Edward Gardner, quoted in Sir Arthur Conan Doyle's *The Coming of the Fairies*

SYLPHS: Air Elementals

Tinker Bell and her flying friends fall into this category of nature spirits. But sylphs aren't just cute and delicate winged beings, as contemporary films and children's books portray them—they handle lots of things related to the air and sky. In addition to possessing the ability to fly, sylphs have the power to manipulate the winds, influence air quality, and help earthlings breathe—some sources say they're busy cleaning up chemtrails these days. They also assist birds and flying insects.

SPRITES: Earth Elementals

Those little green guys you see in the garden are probably sprites (though not all sprites are green or little). Earth elementals include a large cast of characters, such as tree guardians, gnomes, dryads, and some pixies and elves. These nature spirits aid the growth of flowers, trees, and other plants—if you look closely, you might spot them sitting in a tree or resting beneath a blackberry bush. When autumn comes, they change the leaves from green to red, orange, and gold. Earth elementals also play an important role in helping the earth heal from the effects of pollution, deforestation, mining, and other forms of destruction.

The Earth Spirits at Findhorn

In the early 1960s, Eileen and Peter Caddy and their associate Dorothy Maclean founded a spiritual community in a wild and windswept area of northern Scotland known as Findhorn. Even though the soil there was mostly sand and the climate inhospitable, Findhorn became famous for its amazing gardens, which produced tropical flowers and forty-two-pound cabbages. How could this happen? According to Dorothy, the elementals who govern plant growth—she described them as "living forces of creative intelligence that work behind the scene"—guided Findhorn's founders in planting and maintaining the incredible gardens. In his book *Faces of Findhorn*, Professor R. Lindsay Robb of the Soil Association writes, "The vigor, health and bloom of the plants in this garden at mid-winter on land which is almost barren, powdery sand cannot be explained . . ." Well, not by ordinary thinking anyway.

WATER NYMPHS: Water Elementals

Also known as undines, these spirits splash about in the waters of the world. Mermaids fall into this category, too. Usually depicted as beautiful young females, water nymphs perform a variety of tasks, from nourishing life on earth to regulating the tides to inspiring artists and poets. They also protect fish and aquatic creatures and—if they choose—guide humans on sea voyages. In recent times, these elementals have been working hard to offset the effects of water pollution and the destruction of marine habitat.

Shapeshifting Fairies

Although fairies may be members of a particular element, race, or family, many of them can change their appearance when they want to. These "shapeshifters" can transform themselves from grotesque to beautiful, from water beings to flying creatures, or from spirits to animals or even humans. Legends from around the world speak of fairies magically shapeshifting—either out of necessity or when it suits their purposes—into radically different beings, which allows them to go about their business incognito.

Perhaps you've heard of the Irish selkies, or seal people. These enchanted creatures live as seals in the seas, but they can shed their furry pelts and walk on land as humans—they even take mortal mates and produce mixed-breed offspring. In Native American folklore, spirits often assume the shapes of animals and birds, such as coyotes or crows, and Japanese myths speak of a shapeshifting fox called a kitsune. In one of the Brothers Grimm's most intriguing fairy tales, "The Foundling," two siblings transform themselves into numerous forms, including a rose bush, a church, a chandelier, a duck, and a pond, in order to outwit a villain.

So prevalent is shapeshifting among fairies that humans (or other species) may find it difficult to determine with whom they're dealing. Of course, that's part of the fairies' intention.

Where Do Fairies Live?

Even if you can't see them, fairies live nearby. In fact, a fairy might be sitting right beside you or dancing in your yard at this very moment. The reason most people don't see fairies is because they occupy a parallel universe, which exists alongside our own but functions at a different resonance. One way to understand this concept is to compare it to TV or radio channels. When you're watching or listening to one channel, you can't see or hear the others—but they're still there. The same holds true for the land of fairies or the "realm of the fey."

Legends say that fairies went into hiding to avoid the humans who invaded their lands. In some cases, the fairies literally went underground, making their homes in caves, burrows, and underwater fortresses. A folklorist on the Scottish isle of Arran told writer Moyra Doorly that "the fairies left when electricity came." As modern people took over the earth, cutting down trees, building roads, and creating cities, fairy folk withdrew to more remote locales and finally into the spirit world.

An invisible "veil" separates the world of humans from the fairy realm, which makes it challenging for us to interact with them. At certain times of the year—specifically on Beltane (May 1) and Samhain Eve (October 31)—that veil thins, enabling people to see and communicate more easily with spirits of all kinds. Midsummer's Eve, as Shakespeare tells us, is another good time to cavort with the fey.

Fairy Sightings

One summer day in 1947, five-year-old Nona Rees and her mother were walking home from the beach at the seaside community of St. David's in Pembrokeshire, Wales, when they spotted a fairy. Their path led along the rocky coast and through the beautiful countryside—a perfect setting for nature spirits to frolic. According to Nona, they saw "a tiny pure white creature, with wings, like the traditional Christmas Tree fairy but perhaps only an inch to an inch and a half high" above a gorse bush. Being natural history enthusiasts, she and her mother realized it wasn't a moth or butterfly, "it was definitely a fairy."—from *Fairies: Real Encounters with the Little People*, by Janet Bord.

Fairies in Nature

As we've already discussed, fairies serve as nature's caretakers. Mythology tells us that long before humans dominated the landscape, fairies of all kinds populated the earth's wild places. The Welsh Tylwyth Teg, for instance, lived deep in the woods and on isolated islands off the coast of Wales. Germany's nixies dwelt in secret regions beneath streams and waterfalls. The Hungarian tündér perched high on mountaintops. Perhaps these beings were more substantial and less ephemeral in those days than they are now.

Deep in Russia's immense forests, known as the taiga, woodland fairies ruled supreme. These nature spirits, called leshiye, were master shapeshifters who sometimes appeared as tall as trees or as tiny as mice. They could assume the forms of animals or human beings, too, or as composite creatures with green beards and hair and the horns and hooves of a goat. These trickster fairies were known for confusing mortals who intruded into their territory, causing them to become hopelessly lost in leshiye land. Whether the fairies did this for amusement or to safeguard the forests and wildlife from woodcutters and hunters is unknown—perhaps both are true.

Fairies still abide in lakes and mountains, forests and fields. You might also find them flourishing in flower gardens and vegetable patches. They still take seriously their role as nature's stewards, nurturing and protecting not only plants, but stones, animals, and other creatures as well. Many fairies, legends tell us, also possess magical healing powers and excel in the use of herbs and minerals to cure ills of all kinds.

Flower Remedies

In the 1930s, English physician Edward Bach established a holistic form of healing that used flowers to aid a variety of emotional conditions. His thirty-eight original remedies incorporated the vital energy or essence of flowers, diluted in a water-and-brandy solution. To extract the flowers' power, he suspended the blossoms in spring water and set them in the sunshine, which infused the water with their vitality. Despite the lack of physical plant material (Bach just used the flowers' energetic resonance and healing properties), his remedies have proved effective in treating conditions such as stress, depression, insomnia, and anxiety. Is their healing magic rooted in fairy wisdom and the influences of the nature spirits known as devas operating in the plant world?

Usually, fairies stay out of sight of humans, going about their business without fanfare. But if you detour off the beaten track and into the peaceful, unspoiled places on our planet, you may get lucky and enjoy a close encounter with these nature spirits. Just be careful not to get too close or to fall for their ruses—you might never come back from the fairy realm!

LIMINAL ZONES: Thresholds Between Worlds

The slice of seacoast between low and high tides, the deepening foliage between field and forest, the sloping land between plain and mountain—these in-between places are known as liminal zones. Dawn and dusk, the times between day and night, fall into this category, too. Neither wholly one thing nor the other, they serve as bridges that lead from one realm into another. Because of their transient nature, their ambiguity, and their sense of mystery, liminal zones are often the best places to meet fairies and to experience magic.

FAIRY DOORS

In ancient times, fairy doors were portals between the realm of the fairies and the human world. Most of the time, mortals are denied access to fairyland. But at certain times of the year, people could catch a glimpse of the spirit world through these openings. A fairy door might resemble a pathway through a heavily wooded area, a narrow entrance into a cave, a gap in a stone wall, or a knothole in an ancient tree. Shamanic journeys sometimes begin with entering portals such as these in order to visit unseen worlds.

"Come away, O human child!
To the waters and the wild
With a faery, hand in hand,
For the world's more full of weeping than you can understand."

— W.B. Yeats, *The Collected Poems*

Ann Arbor's Fairy Doors

• •

In April 2005, an architectural anomaly—a miniature door—mysteriously showed up near the entrance of a coffee shop in Ann Arbor, Michigan. Over the next year and a half, nine more little doors—dubbed "fairy doors"—materialized at various locations throughout the city. These handsome entryways, usually no more than a foot high, are believed to have been created by artist and children's book author Jonathan B. Wright, perhaps as a way to alert humans to the presence of fairies in urban environments or to give urban fairies access to art galleries, boutiques, and other interesting places throughout the city. Since that time, some of the establishments have closed and the fairy doors have disappeared as well. But that doesn't mean they're gone for good—who knows when another fairy door might appear, perhaps in a location near you. To view these tiny treasures, visit Wright's website, *www.urban-fairies.com*.

Demoted Deities

Many folklorists believe that fairies descended from ancient gods and goddesses. For thousands of years, these deities had dominion over the earth, the heavens, and all the inhabitants therein. They governed day and night, land and water, the seasons, the growth of plants, wild and domestic animals—just about everything. Their all-encompassing powers made them awesome beings indeed, and people in virtually every culture around the world worshipped some sort of divine ruler(s).

But the rise of Christianity coincided with the decline of many early gods and goddesses. The Church not only discouraged belief in the old ways, it persecuted people who clung to them. Legend tells us that when people stopped honoring and paying homage to the old gods and goddesses, their powers began to wane. Consequently, some deities were demoted to mythical beings—including fairies. This development didn't exactly please the fairies, which might be why they play tricks on humans.

Like everywhere else, the fairy realm has its social structure and hierarchies. Basically, fairies can be grouped into two categories:

1. Those who guard and guide the natural world
2. Those who deal with destiny and the fate of humankind

The Fairies of Fate

We've already talked a bit about the nature spirits; now let's take a look at the fairies of fate. These beings often show up shortly after an infant's birth to celebrate and to influence the baby's destiny. Usually they bring gifts to the newborn, such as courage or beauty or cleverness. These birth spirits make appearances in Celtic, Slavic, and French folklore. The Greek Moirae or Fates also fall into this category. So do the Albanian fatit, except they generally wait until the third day after the baby's birth to visit, when they fly in on the backs of butterflies. In Serbia, fairies called oosood arrive seven days after the birth but only show themselves to the new mother.

It's a good idea to offer the fairies something in return for their generosity; otherwise they may take offense—and it's never a good idea to dis a fairy! Traditionally, the parents of the newborn throw a feast for the fairies to thank them and to encourage their assistance in the future. In typical French fashion, Breton spirits enjoy champagne with their meal. A wise parent will give the Seven Hathors, the daughters and/or companion spirits associated with the Egyptian goddess Hathor, red ribbons in addition to food.

On her website *www.fairysource.com*, Bernadette Wulf says, "It is my belief that we need to reconnect with faerie, plant, animal, and mineral beings in mutual respect in order to restore harmony and balance to our minds and bodies, as well as healing to the many areas of our planet that we have damaged."

Sleeping Beauty's Fairy Godmothers

In Charles Perrault's famous fairy tale, *La Belle au bois dormant* ("Sleeping Beauty"), a king and queen invite seven fairies to be godmothers to their new daughter. However, they forget about another important fairy, who becomes angry at the oversight. After six of the fairies have presented their gifts, the irate fairy places a curse on the baby: She'll prick her finger while spinning and die. The last fairy godmother, however, softens the girl's fate so that instead of dying the girl will fall into an enchanted sleep for 100 years, until wakened by a prince's kiss. The Brothers Grimm later adapted the tale for German readers and called it "Little Briar Rose."

"We find in most countries a popular belief in different classes of beings distinct from men, and from the higher orders of divinities. These beings are usually believed to inhabit, in the caverns of the earth, or the depths of the waters, a region of their own. They generally excel mankind in power and in knowledge, and like them are subject to the inevitable laws of earth, though after a more prolonged period of existence."

—Thomas Keightley, *Fairy Mythology*

CHAPTER 2

Fairy Characteristics

What image comes to mind when you think about fairies? Dainty female figures with gossamer wings, long flowing hair, and gauzy dresses? Maybe waving magic wands or flinging sparkly pixie dust around? Most likely they're tiny enough to perch on flower petals, but regardless of size these magical creatures are always dazzlingly gorgeous—and sometimes sexy, in an ephemeral sort of way. Of course, they're also sweet, fun-loving beings, just the sort of playmates you'd like your kids to hang out with.

Nice, but not true—unless you're in Disneyland, that is.

The Good, the Bad, the Beautiful, and the Downright Ugly

Until the last century or so, fairies came in a wide assortment of sizes, shapes, and colors—with a variety of temperaments to match. Yes, indeed, some were exquisitely beautiful, but others could star in your worst nightmare. And when it came to their behavior, parental guidance was definitely advised.

In the previous chapter, we touched on some of the features of the fairy folk from various legends and lands, but now let's get better acquainted with some of the most popular fairies.

PIXIES

Early legends describe pixies as small, childlike beings who live beneath stone circles and fairy mounds in and around the British Isles and Brittany—although some say they may have Swedish ancestry because the Swedes call them pyske. Pixies have also been linked with the Picts, a race of mysterious, small, dark people who occupied Ireland and northern Britain in ancient times. For the most part, pixies are considered "good guys" in the fairy world—nature spirits who not only tend to plants but also sometimes help people with domestic chores. They're quite fond of riding horses as well. Although usually harmless and playful, pixies enjoy a bit of mischief now and again.

Contemporary pixies generally sport pointed ears and green garb, including tall, pointed hats. But J.K. Rowling, in *Harry Potter and the Chamber of Secrets*, depicts them as blue trickster-types about eight inches tall. In the Artemis Fowl novels, author Eoin Colfer portrays them as greedy and cunning, though traditional fairy tales present a more positive image.

ELVES

Today the word "elves" conjures up images of Santa's little help-ers, but early folklore describes them as handsome, human-size beings. They show up in the legends of the Teutonic peoples, where the elves exhibit great skill as artisans, archers, and healers. Scandinavian myths divide elves into three types. Light Elves dwell with the gods and god-desses in the Upper World. Dark Elves live in the Lower World. Black Elves are attractive and human in size and live in a realm between the other two. According to Norse folklore, humans who proved them-selves worthy could advance to the level of elves after death.

Shakespeare sometimes used the terms "elves" and "fairies" inter-changeably. Folklorists might argue that elves could be considered a subset within the generic species called "fairies," but they form a distinct group unto themselves. In *A Midsummer Night's Dream*, the Bard presents them as small, mischievous beings. Hans Christian Andersen, in his fairy tale "The Elf of the Rose," described elves as

being small enough to live inside a rose. J.R.R. Tolkien, in *Lord of the Rings*, however, portrayed elves as a noble race, tall, handsome, and benevolent, resistant to disease and death.

Tradition says elves don't much like humans and can harm as well as help people—despite the fact that elves have been known to mate with mortals, as did the mother of the warrior Hogni, one of the last survivors after the fall of the Germanic *Nibelungen*. Stories tell of these spirits attacking humans with poisoned darts known as "elf-shot." And in "The Elfin Hill," Andersen writes that the pretty females of the species, who love music and dancing, have been know to spin about so deliriously that they dance human men to death.

Icelandic Elves

The people of Iceland have a special relationship with elves, closer perhaps than citizens of any other culture. Iceland's Tourist Board reports that 80 percent of the country's people believe elves exist. Iceland has even enacted policies to protect the elves from human incursion. In the port city of Hafnarfjordur, where 25 percent of residents say they've seen fairies, land has been preserved for the elves and no construction can take place in designated areas. People who fear they've offended the elves by building on their sacred ground may call in an elf-whisperer to meet with the elves and find a way to resolve the problem.

DWARFS

You're probably familiar with the seven dwarfs in the story of Snow White. In Disney's animated movie, these funny little guys have names that represent an array of human temperaments: Happy,

Grumpy, Sleepy, and so on. Like Snow White's companions, dwarfs in fairy lore tend to be bearded folk who, despite their short stature, are surprisingly strong. Even though they sport bushy beards, they may be no more than seven years old—these fellows mature fast!

Dwarfs and trolls share a number of characteristics in Norse and Germanic mythology—in some cases, the terms are used interchangeably. Both species live underground in magnificent structures hidden beneath the hills. Both excel at metalsmithing, and both are said to possess great wealth. Early folklore linked dwarfs with the dead, suggesting that they hung around burial grounds. The ancient Norse epic *Poetic Edda* says the King of the Dwarfs was "shaped from the blood of fire and the limbs of the dead."

TROLLS

Trolls get mixed reviews in legends and folklore, and their image seems to have deteriorated over the centuries. Some fairy tales describe them as friendly and even helpful to mortals, but other stories say trolls have a sinister side, too—they're thieves who steal not only property, but human women and children as well. Of course, they have magical powers, including the ability to make themselves invisible or to shapeshift into other forms.

Usually these creatures appear as ugly, dull-witted, hunched-over creatures. J.R.R. Tolkien's tales of Middle-earth present them as huge, humanlike beasts with a peculiar weakness: when exposed to sunlight, they turn to stone. However, early legends describe trolls as fierce yet comely (especially the females).

Trolls love music and dancing, as most fairies do, and they've been known to go to great lengths to bring music into their lands. Of course, they couldn't just download tunes, so they kidnapped human musicians to entertain them and held the musicians as prisoners. Some tales, such as Ursula LeGuin's "A Ride on the Red Mare's Back," cast trolls in an even darker light as mountain folk who abduct children.

Despite their unsavory reputations in modern literature, trolls in old stories are often portrayed as benevolent. These nocturnal beings live underground, in burrows or caves, where they guard vast stores of treasure. They're especially skillful at working with herbs and metals, and sometimes willingly aid mortals. Like many fairy folk, they excel at shapeshifting and spellcasting, which can confuse humans who come across them.

HAGS

These fairies look like old women, and the term is often used interchangeably for spirits as well as for human crones with magical powers. Folklore often holds them responsible for nightmares, and some stories say they sit on sleeping men's chests, causing a feeling of immobility known as sleep paralysis. In other tales, hags transform themselves into beautiful young women and sneak into men's bedrooms at night as succubi to have sex with sleeping mortals.

Hags turn up in the myths of many cultures, as the Irish banshee (*bean sidhe*), Eastern Europe's Baba Yaga, and Japan's Onibaba. Perhaps the most familiar hags in the English-speaking world are the three witches in Shakespeare's *Macbeth*, who chant "toil and trouble" while stirring their strange brew. Although folklore acknowledges their powers as healers, sometimes linking hags with Hecate and the nature goddesses of winter, neither mythology nor modern literature has much good to say about these beings. Like witches, hags for centuries have been portrayed almost universally as ugly, evil creatures who consort with the devil and other demonic forces. This misconception may have contributed to the murders of countless human women and children in Europe and the American colonies from the fifteenth through the eighteenth centuries.

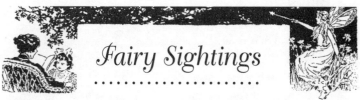

Fairy Sightings

In *The Traveller's Guide to Fairy Sites*, Janet Bord records the story of an English woman's encounter with a fairy. "When we were on holiday in Cornwall my daughter and I came down a winding lane, and all of a sudden there was a small green man by a gate watching us. All in green, with a pointed hood and ears . . . We were cold with terror. We ran for the ferry below . . . I don't think I have ever been so frightened."

LEPRECHAUNS

Legend says if you capture a leprechaun he'll give you a pot of gold—but if you think you can con a leprechaun out of his treasure, think again. These seemingly guileless guys are much too clever to let humans snatch their gold from them easily. In folklore, these Irish tricksters usually show themselves as little old men about three feet tall, sometimes wearing funny hats and green coats, smoking briar pipes, and carrying shillelaghs. Most of them work as cobblers and, like many Irishmen, they enjoy a bit of fun and a spot of drink at the end of the day.

Neither good nor bad, leprechauns are capricious fellows who like to play practical jokes. Legend says they must grant you three wishes if you catch them, but be careful what you ask for! Often they do good turns for humans and might even bring you good luck—if it suits them, that is. It's rumored that leprechauns descended from the powerful Tuatha dé Danann (the divine ancestors of the Irish race), but popular culture has diminished them to little more than jolly imps who tuck four-leaf clovers in their lapels and drink green beer on St. Patrick's Day.

GOBLINS

Ugly and mean-spirited, these small creatures often travel in groups and wreak havoc—they're the fairy equivalent of human gangs. According to some accounts, these greedy guys love money and other goodies, and they're not above using trickery or other means to get what they want. If Pierre Dubois's account of them in *The Complete Encyclopedia of Elves, Goblins, and Other Little Creatures* is accurate, they have no real home and end up taking shelter where they can find it, in the roots of trees or in cracks between rocks, which may account for their surly nature.

In some folktales they're portrayed as little meanies who aren't very smart, with greenish skin or hairy bodies and red eyes. In Eoin

The Hobgoblin laughed till his sides ached

Coffer's Artemis Fowl series, they resemble lizards. Their short stature (only about three feet tall) may contribute to their need to prove their virility by behaving aggressively. Some legends describe them as more mischievous than dangerous—the sort of pranksters who might wake you up during the night by banging pots—although they've also been said to steal babies or dig up graves and toss the bones around. J.K. Rowling's goblins are greedy and arrogant, but also quite shrewd. (Hobgoblins, on the other hand, tend to behave better.)

THE SIDHE

According to Irish mythology, the sidhe (pronounced *shee*) are an ancient and powerful group of spirits who've occupied Ireland and parts of Scotland since before recorded history. The word translates as "people of the hills," for the sidhe live underground in fairy mounds and beneath fairy rings. Also known as aos sí, aes sidhe, and other names, they may be descended from the Tuatha dé Danann.

Though humanlike in appearance, the sidhe are usually described as exquisitely beautiful, with powers far exceeding those of mortals. They can fly through the air at great speeds, for instance, and can transform themselves into other creatures. Legend also says these fairies are nearly immortal. Even after Christianity moved into Celtic lands, the Irish and Scots continued to hold these supernatural beings in high esteem. (We'll talk more about the sidhe in Chapter 7: Ireland's Feyfolk.)

Animal Fairies

Animals can be fairies—and fairies can be animals. In fact, shapeshifting spirits love to change themselves into animals, birds, and even reptiles. Because fairies serve as guardians for the natural world, they form close friendships with animals—including enchanted creatures such as unicorns and dragons.

Myths and legends from around the world speak of animal fairies as well as animal-human hybrids. For instance, South Africa's tokolosh is said to look like a small, tailless baboon. The Irish selkies live as seals in the ocean but come on land as humans. The encantado of Brazil can turn themselves into snakes or dolphins. Japanese yosei show up as swans or cranes, and the Welsh gwyllion sometimes assume goat forms. Like other fairies, animal spirits may behave in a kindly or hostile manner toward humans.

NATIVE AMERICAN SPIRIT ANIMALS

Among the indigenous tribes of North and South America you'll find myriad stories of magical entities in the forms of animals, birds, reptiles, and insects. Some sources say that spirit animals are actually supernatural beings who at times inhabit the bodies of animals. Other sources explain that these beings once walked the earth as flesh-and-blood animals, but when they died they became divine. Regardless of where they originated, these creatures can teach humans a lot. Native American traditions regard spirit animals highly and honor them as guardians of the people. (For more information, please see my book *The Secret Power of Spirit Animals*.)

BLACK DOGS OF BRITAIN

Throughout the British Isles and Ireland, people claim to have seen shaggy black canines as big as calves. These animals are known to haunt churches, old roads, and historic sites. Folklore links these black dogs with death, and when you see one it's a sure sign that someone is about to die. According to author Katharine Briggs, these mythic creatures may be ghosts of dogs, ghosts of humans, or demons.

A type of fairy called a bogie often shows up as a black dog. When someone dies, legend says he calls out to all the hounds in the town and they go barking together through the streets. The Scots say black dogs also stand guard over treasure in places such as Perthshire. These folktales likely contributed to the inspiration for Sir Arthur Conan Doyle's story "The Hound of the Baskervilles."

CELTIC CATS

The ancient Egyptians revered cats as deities, but the Celts also attributed supernatural powers to felines. In Irish folklore, cat sidhe guard access to the Underworld and its treasure. Magical white cats accompany the Welsh goddess Ceridwen. Images of cats, put there by an ancient race known as the Picts, appear on special stones in Scotland. Female fairies and witches have long been known to keep cats as familiars (magical companions) and to shapeshift into cats.

Fairy Sightings

On the morning of August 4, 1577, a terrifying storm shook a church in Bungay, Suffolk, England, frightening the parishioners. Suddenly a black dog raced through the church. It passed one man, who died on the spot; another was badly burned. Today, a weathervane in Bungay Market reminds people of the eerie event.

ENCHANTED HORSES

Unicorns, centaurs, and flying horses delight young and old alike—but folklore, art, and literature also tell us that seemingly ordinary horses may be enchanted beings as well. Considering fairies' fascination with all things equine, it's no surprise to find horses in fairyland, and fairies posing as horses. Scotland's water spirits known as kelpies often shapeshift into horses. The German nix, also a water fairy, is said to transform himself into a gray horse. Perhaps these mythical beings inspired German artist Walter Crane to paint his famous *Neptune's Pferde* (*The Horses of Neptune*) in 1893—the majestic white horses emerging from the ocean in the picture certainly look magical.

The vila of Eastern Europe can transform themselves into horses, too, as well as swans and wolves. Phooka (var: Pooka), an Irish goblin, sometimes takes the shape of a black dog, sometimes a horse. Don't accept a ride from him, though—he'll take you on a wild romp and then dump you in the mud. But the most gruesome and grotesque fairy-horse is the Scots' nuckalavee. This horrifying version of a centaur has a single, red eye and flippers instead of hooves. Worse yet, it lacks skin—its red muscles and black-blooded veins are clearly visible.

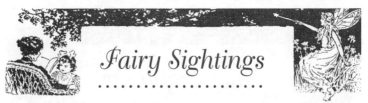

Fairy Sightings

On Samhain Eve, 1971, Herbie Brennan, Irish author of the Faerie Wars series of books, and his friend Jim Henry decided to visit an ancient mystical site known as the Longstone Rath, an earthenware ring surrounding an eighteen-foot-tall stone megalithic. Shortly before midnight, says Brennan, two dozen white horses "no bigger than cocker spaniels" suddenly galloped across the structure, then disappeared, sending the two startled men running from the scene.

FROG PRINCES

In one of the Brothers Grimm's best-known fairy tales, "The Frog Prince," a princess meets an enchanted frog who's really a prince and frees him from an imprisoning spell cast upon him by an angry fairy. In the original story, the princess reluctantly lets the frog eat from her plate and sleep on her pillow. In later, romanticized versions the princess overcomes her revulsion and kisses the frog, which breaks the spell. Similar stories of slimy suitors appear in the folklore of many countries, including "The Maiden and the Frog" (England) and "The Frog Prince" (Sri Lanka). Disney brought out an animated film version of Grimm's fairy tale titled *The Princess and the Frog* in 1992—the moral is don't judge a book by its cover.

"I believe in everything until it's disproved. So I believe in fairies, the myths, dragons. It all exists, even if it's in your mind. Who's to say that dreams and nightmares aren't as real as the here and now?"

—John Lennon

CHAPTER 3

Fairy Behavior and Misbehavior

arge or small, handsome or heinous, fairies both fascinate and frighten us. We want to believe in them, to befriend them, but we've heard rumors that make us just a little bit wary. As we've already read, fairies play pranks on humans, cause them to get lost in the woods, or steal things—they've even been known to drown men and kidnap babies. Still, we're drawn to them like moths to a flame. Perhaps their unpredictability and the challenges they pose for mortals make them all the more alluring. Maybe it's time to examine some of the conflicting stories about fairies and get to know these charismatic creatures better. If we learn which ones to welcome into our lives and which ones to steer clear of, we can avoid calamities and enjoy the good fortune the fairies offer people.

Fairy Power

Myths and legends tell us that fairies have an arsenal of supernatural powers that they can use for good or ill—and mere mortals are no match for them. Throughout history, friendly fairies have helped humans by protecting crops and livestock, healing the sick and delivering babies, granting wishes and bringing good luck. Angry spirits, on the other hand, reportedly stir up storms, wither crops, conjure plagues, cast curses that last for eternity, and turn humans into toads, stones, or worse. So obviously, you want to stay in the fairies' good graces.

But here's the conundrum. Fairies don't feel emotions the way humans do, nor do they share our sense of ethics—although they have their own codes, which can be quite rigid. At best, fairies could be considered amoral. Our ancestors sought to understand the ways of the fey in order to win the fairies' favor and avoid incurring their wrath. You might want to do the same, because even though these spirits seem pretty innocuous in the way they're depicted by modern media, they have a long tradition of being anything but. Let's start by looking at some of the special powers fairies possess.

FAIRIES LIVE PRACTICALLY FOREVER

They may not be immortal, but fairies live a whole lot longer than humans do—ten times as long, maybe more. According to some legends, they populated the planet eons before people came on the scene. During all those millennia, they've had time to learn every-thing there is to know about mortals. Furthermore, as fairies age they hold onto their powers instead of growing feeble and senile like humans.

Fairies Don't Need Facelifts

In the bestseller *Artemis Fowl: The Arctic Incident*, elfin Holly Short, despite her youthful face and figure, is actually an octogenarian. But she's a mere kid in com-parison to some characters in the book—one of the dwarfs is reputedly 2,000 years old.

FAIRIES ARE STRONGER THAN THEY LOOK

Many fairy tales tell of giants and other monsters, such as the huge and hairy Norse trolls who look sort of like Bigfoot (with Bigfoot's characteristic foul odor as well). But even little dwarfs pack some muscle—they're adults by the age of three. In Hawaiian mythol-ogy, small spirits called the menehuene supposedly created amazing stone dams and walls on the island of Kauai, and Arabic myths say fairies known as the jinn built the pyramids.

FAIRIES CAN FORETELL THE FUTURE

Not only do many fairies have keener vision than humans, they can see into the future. "The Sight" (clairvoyance) is natural to them, so they know what's going to happen before it does. Obviously, this eliminates guesswork and gives them the upper hand in most situations.

Fairy Foresight

. . . .

An old Irish legend tells of a warrior named Teigue, son of a lord of Munster, who embarked on a mission of revenge against an invader named Cathmann who'd captured Teigue's wife and brothers. Along the way, Teigue met a fairy woman who told him when and how he would die many years hence. Her vision allowed Teigue to pursue his enemy without fear.

FAIRIES CAN MAKE THEMSELVES INVISIBLE

Now you see her, now you don't. Just when you finally think you've spotted a fairy, she throws a cloak of invisibility over her shoulders and vanishes before your very eyes. Maybe she simply merged quietly into the shadows or greenery around her, or she might have slipped back through the veil that separates the land of enchantment from our own. The truth is, you'll only see a fairy if she wants you to. What's more, fairies can cause their entire kingdoms to appear and disappear in the blink of an eye, leaving you wondering if you dreamed the whole thing.

Glamour Spells

. . . .

A fairy is likely to have a charm in her bag of tricks called a "glamour spell." This enables her to show herself to humans in a favorable light and thus win them over. An evil or disgusting-looking fairy can appear beautiful, trustworthy, or kind—anything she chooses, in order to trick unwitting mortals. The German nixie is famous for doing this. Glamour—when and whether to use it—is a major concern for Neil Gaiman's fairy Nuala in the *Sandman* series. Magical tradition says human beings can learn the art of casting glamour spells, too, but that's a subject for another book.

What Do Fairies Do for Fun?

Like humans, fairies enjoy eating, drinking, music, and dancing. When the day's work of protecting the fields and forests, mining underground caves, or wreaking havoc in the human world is done, fairies just want to have fun.

DANCING AND SINGING FAIRIES

Fairies love to dance, according to folklore and literature. Countless tales speak of these spirits cavorting in the moonlight, skipping and spinning in dewy meadows and forest glades—sometimes in small groups, but sometimes by the hundreds. A Cornish story says 600 pixies once gathered to dance in a huge circle at Cornwall's Trevose Head. In *A Midsummer Night's Dream*, Shakespeare writes that fairies congregate:

> *"On hill, in dale, forest or mead,*
>
> *By paved fountain, or by rushy brook,*
>
> *Or on the beached margent of the sea,*
>
> *To dance their ringlets to the whistling wind."*

Shakespeare's contemporaries also found dancing fairies a delightful topic for drama. Either John Lyly or John Day (the author is unknown) penned the following verse in *The Maydes Metamorphosis*:

> *"By the moon we sport and play,*
>
> *With the night begins our day;*

As we dance the dew doth fall—

Trip it, little urchins all,

Lightly as the little bee,

Two by two, and three by three;

And about go we, and about go we."

Not all fairies, however, dance purely for the fun of it—some have other agendas. The vila of Eastern Europe use dance as a form of enchantment to attract men and seduce them. The Russian rusalki go even further. These water spirits live in rivers by day, but at night they transform themselves into beautiful young women and come ashore. There these lusty ladies dance and sing to entice human males, then lure the men back to the rivers and drown them. Legend says that once Hungary's tündér take human men as dance partners they won't let them go until the men fall ill from exhaustion or die. Wales's Tylwyth Teg love music so much they've been known to kidnap human musicians and keep them imprisoned in fairyland forever, so the fairies can have music all the time.

FAIRY FEASTS

Food plays a role in the world's social traditions and celebrations— dining and companionship are a winning combination, whether you're a human or a fairy. What do fairies like to eat? It varies, depending on where they live. Breton fairies (like the French people) enjoy lavish feasts complete with wine and pastries. Greek dryads like wine, too, but also milk and honey—and don't forget the olive oil. Senegal's yumboes are especially fond of fish. The ellyllon of Wales eat toadstools. Garden fairies, naturally, prefer flower nectar or wild berries.

The Iranian peri don't eat at all—they get the nourishment they need from merely smelling flowers.

Bread, that staple in the human world, gets mixed reviews from fairies. Celtic spirits and Britain's brownies like bread, but in Newfoundland people use bread to ward off fairies. The dwarfs in J.R.R. Tolkien's fantasy books eat a nourishing but rather hard and tasteless bread called "cram." Another type of bread known as "lembas" was a specialty among the elves, who kept their recipe secret. Drinking the elfin elixir miruvor (perhaps brewed from honey and flower nectar) boosted the elves' vim and vigor, whereas the magical Ent-draught had the power to heal wounds and make hobbits grow taller.

Modern-day fairies, however, might turn up their little noses at traditional elfin bread. Instead, serve them soft, white "fairy bread" cut into fun shapes, spread with butter, and decorated with colorful sprinkles.

Early fairy tales were told by peasants—subsistence farmers, fishermen, and hunters who lived a hand-to-mouth existence. In many parts of the world, hunger and poverty still prevail. So perhaps it's no surprise that stories often involve enchanted food and/or cooking tools. Ireland's Tuatha dé Dannan, for instance, owned magic cauldrons that were never empty. In the story by the Brothers Grimm, "Table-Be-Set, Gold-Donkey, and Cudgel Out of the Sack," a magic table provides ample food for everyone. Of course, wicked fairies used food for evil purposes—Snow White's poisoned apple, for example, and the gingerbread house in "Hansel and Gretel."

What should you do if a fairy invites you to dinner? Most legends advise you to decline. Eating with the fairies is the fastest and surest way to get trapped in their realm forever!

Fairy Tale Feasts

In their charming illustrated cookbook *Fairy Tale Feasts*, the mother-daughter team of Jane Yolen and Heidi Stemple introduce young readers to the history of foods in fairy tales. Through the collection of stories and recipes, the authors inspire children to use their own talents to combine the arts of cooking and storytelling.

SPORTING FAIRIES

Every land has its favorite sports and games—and the fairy world is no exception. Horseback riding is particularly popular with the pixies, who steal horses for clandestine canters during the night.

While living in England, shortly before bowling was introduced into the United States from the UK, Washington Irving wrote his famous story "Rip Van Winkle." In it, a man comes upon a group of short, bearded fellows in New York's Catskill Mountains playing ninepins. After drinking some of their liquor, Rip falls asleep and wakes up twenty years later. Quite likely Rip's companions were dwarfs or trolls, and he fell into a common fairy trap: He drank with them and ended up lost for an extended period of time in their hidden realm in the mountains.

As interest in girls' sports has grown, fairies have gotten into athletics. Author Daisy Meadows's *Rainbow Magic* series of books features youthful sporting fairies, including Helena the horseback-riding fairy, Gemma the gymnast, and Stacey the soccer star. Not surprisingly, in these fanciful, modern-day fairy tales goblins play the bad guys, who steal the fairy athletes' magical objects and threaten to upset the entire fairy Olympics.

Fairy Sightings

An article published in the UK's *Bridport News* (December 3, 2009) reported that throughout rural Britain people were discovering their horses' manes and tails mysteriously braided. Harriet Laurie of the Shipton Riding Club, who found unexplained braids in the mane of her horse Stormy, told the newspaper, "There has been an absolute furore whipping up about plaits in horses' manes." Dozens of horses met the same fate, but no one could figure out who did it, or how—the stealthy braiders even managed to sneak by guard dogs. Could fairies be responsible? Police, however, attributed it to the pagan spell-casting practice known as "knot magic" and noted that no horses were injured or stolen.

Fairy Fashions

Tinker Bell flits about in her cute strapless green mini-dress with its leafy skirt. Holly Short tries to appear a bit tougher in her tight-fitting green body suit. But what do real fairies wear? That depends on where and when they live, who they are, and what they do—the same as in the human world.

- ❖ The commoners among the Welsh Tylwyth Teg are said to wear green, but the royal members of the species dress in red and blue silk.
- ❖ The vila of Eastern Europe prefer white, sheer gowns.
- ❖ The kachina of the American Southwest don elaborately beaded clothing made from deerskin.
- ❖ England's brownies dress humbly in worn, brown work duds.
- ❖ Leprechauns prefer green garb, funny hats, leather aprons, and shoes with large buckles.

- Green clothes are a favorite with pixies, too.
- The Irish trooping fairies often dress up in elegant attire and jewelry like that worn in the Medieval and Renaissance royal courts, whereas the solitary fairies prefer to clothe themselves in moss, cobwebs, leaves, and flowers.
- Ireland's merrows are known for their red caps, which enable them to live underwater—if a mortal steals a merrow's cap, he can prevent her from returning to the sea.
- Redcap, one of the most evil characters in British folklore, sports a red hat, too—dyed with human blood. He takes up residence in places where blood has been shed and kills unsuspecting passersby.
- Members of the modern fantasy-fiction elfin race known as the Tel'quessir adopt a variety of looks based on tribal, warrior, and futuristic motifs.

Today's fairy fashions range from darling tutu-like dresses to elegant velvet or hand-painted silk gowns to glow-in-the-dark X-rated outfits designed to fuel succubus fantasies.

However, one major distinction separates fairy garb from that of humans: Fairy clothes are enchanted. Fairy garments don't just protect the wearer from the elements or flatter her figure—they give her magical powers. In Taiwanese folklore the nadjeni use vests covered with fish scales so they can live underwater. The nineteenth-century Irish poet Lady Wilde wrote about strange little men who wore white tunics that enabled them to fly. Greek mythology describes a helmet called the Helm of Darkness that makes both humans and spirits invisible. Legends from the Far East, Britain, and Native American nations speak of cloaks that confer invisibility—an idea J.K. Rowling borrowed for the Harry Potter books.

"I think that people who can't believe in fairies aren't worth knowing."

—Tori Amos, American pianist, singer, and composer

CHAPTER 4

Fairy Relationships with Humans

O ur modern-day fascination with fairies is nothing new. If we scratch the surface of virtually any culture's mythology, we'll find a fabulous body of fairy lore. Some myths say fairies preceded us on earth by eons, and we've coexisted with them—albeit not always harmoniously—since people first set foot on Planet Earth. According to Irish legend, the fairies known as the Tuatha dé Dannan were the ancestors of the Irish race. Cambodians believe they descended from spirits called nagas and naginis. The ancient Romans revered nature spirits, i.e., fairies, even before they began worshipping gods and goddesses. Greek mythology says that a nymph raised Zeus, the head honcho of the Greek pantheon. Jewish legend tells us that Adam and Eve birthed fairies called the mazikeen. Might this mean that we all have a bit of fairy blood in us?

How Fairies View Humans

Today, most of us don't think of fairies as having any impact on our daily existence. If we think about them at all, it's as trifling cartoon characters that amuse our kids. But until about a century or so ago, humans viewed fairies as powerful, supernatural beings who held the high cards in the game of life. If mortals wanted to succeed—or even survive—they needed to placate the fairies. These otherworldly beings wielded tremendous power over everyday events as well as human life and death, and being capricious sorts, they might just as well destroy a person as lend him a hand. Woe be to those who crossed a fairy—doom and gloom would surely dog their future.

Truth be told, most fairies don't like mortals and never have. They consider humans an inferior race. From the fairies' perspective, we need them—they don't need us. According to some legends, humans invaded the world of the fey and forced the spirits underground, which didn't exactly engender positive feelings among the fairies. But contemporary people don't realize this. Consequently, we don't show the fairies the respect they think they deserve, which means our chances of gaining their assistance are practically nil. Furthermore, as the keepers of nature, the fairies are understandably angry with us for polluting the earth, plundering her resources, and carving up her body for our own benefit.

Because fairies occupy a realm that abuts the human one, we can't avoid coming in contact with one another occasionally. In some ways, our interests align.

Like neighbors in any community, we must learn to live amicably side by side. Familiarizing ourselves with fairies is the first step toward developing cooperation, for the good of all concerned.

Fairy and Human Relations Congress

Since the year 2000, hundreds of people and thousands of fairies have met annually at the Skalitude Retreat Center in Twisp, Washington, to explore, deepen, and improve human relationships with the natural world and the spirits who occupy it. On the Congress's website (*www.fairycongress.com*) Michael Pilarski writes, "The fairy beings who attend the Fairy Congress are fully as intelligent (and often much more so) than the human participants. We approach the fairies and devas with respect and love as co-creators of this event. . . . It is a rare event for humans to experience so much fairy energy and such an outpouring of fairy/devic blessings."

Friends or Foes?

Like people, some fairies are good guys and some are bad news. Although fairies play both roles in the lives of humans, they're notoriously unpredictable—legends warn that we can't rely on even the most benevolent fairies to behave nicely toward us all the time. These sensitive creatures can change faster than the weather, and they're certainly not to be toyed with. For instance, the usually shy and reclusive Middle Eastern jinn can be dangerous if you offend them by uttering their real names. Germany's kobolds sometimes aid miners and sometimes obstruct them. Water spirits known as the Blue Men of the Minch whip up storms and wreck ships—but these fairies enjoy a good rhyme and if any poets are onboard they may be spared. Scotland's female glaistigs treat children and the elderly kindly but suck the blood of men.

Early humans associated fairies with fate and feared them, for in the days of old, fate dealt most people hard lives. Therefore, our ancestors sought ways to avoid upsetting the fairies and incurring more problems. Janet Bord, author of *Fairies: Real Encounters with Little People*, explains that for humans, meetings with fairies were usually unintended and unpleasant. "The bad fortune which humans often experienced at the hands of fairies resulted in the widespread use of charms and rituals to try and keep them away."

WHIMSICAL OR WICKED?

Which fairies are whimsical and which are wicked? Let's look at a few of the best and the worst. Of course, within any group (as is true among humans), individual fairies may rise above their unsavory roots or deviate from their amiable families to become reprehensible misfits. Remember, though, that no fairy can ever truly be called a friend—except, perhaps, that darling little Barbie Mariposa doll your daughter adores.

Friendly Fairies

- Scottish brownies assist people with domestic chores, cleaning the house, or plowing the fields after everyone else has gone to bed.
- Native American spirit animals guard and guide humans.
- The Incan huacas protect crops and livestock.
- Irish merrows are known for their gentle and cheerful natures.

Mischievous and Malevolent Fairies

❖ Goblins roam in packs, terrorizing humans and ruining property.

❖ In Hindu mythology, cannibalistic rakshasas eat holy men and cause leprosy.

❖ England's spriggans steal children, rob homes, and damage crops.

❖ India's troublemaking mumiai torment people of the lower castes by attacking them and destroying their belongings and gardens.

❖ The Russian rusalki charm human men, then drown them.

❖ Japanese tengu herald death and war.

Can Fairies Really Grant Wishes?

In stories and movies, fairies simply wave their magic wands or snap their fingers to make a human's wishes instantly come true. In real life, things happen differently—not because the fairies *can't* fulfill a wish in the blink of an eye, but because humans aren't prepared for that. We're not used to getting what we want instantaneously. Instead, fairies today often guide us in achieving our dreams, maybe nudging us in the right direction or giving us helpful insights. But fairy power isn't infinite; they can only grant wishes that fall within the realm of human possibility—so don't ask them to make you sprout wings and fly.

TRICKSTERS AND THIEVES

Fairies like to tease and torment humans. Irish leprechauns are notorious for playing tricks on people, especially those who want to grab the fairies' gold. Pixies confuse travelers, causing them to veer off track and get lost. Britain's bogles sneak into people's houses and mess things up, make strange noises, and generally annoy the occupants.

One of the most common tricks fairies pull on mortals is hiding things or moving ordinary household stuff around. Once, while getting ready for work, I laid my hairbrush down on the bathroom vanity and bent over to retrieve something I'd dropped. When I stood up, the brush had disappeared. A few days later, it "magically" reappeared in exactly the same place I'd set it down. It seems the fairies do this either for their own amusement or to get our attention, because if you ask politely they usually give the objects back. So the next time you lose your keys or glasses, ask the fairies to please return them.

Fairy Sightings

In *The Fairy-Faith in Celtic Countries*, W.Y. Evans-Wentz recounts a strange story of a Welsh farmer who one night discovered a group of little people about a foot tall in his cowshed. The fairies paid no attention to him as they quickly killed and ate his ox. Then, to the man's surprise, they reassembled the ox—all but one tiny bone in the beast's leg—so that it looked quite normal. When the fairies had taken what they wanted, they disappeared. In the morning, the cow seemed perfectly fine, except it limped slightly on the leg that was missing a bone.

John Gregorson Campbell, in *Superstitions of the Highlands and Islands of Scotland*, writes that elves have a reputation as thieves, but they only steal the toradh—the value of a thing—not its actual substance. For example, the elves might leave a cow's body but take away its ability to produce milk.

Changeling Children

Stories of fairies snatching human children abound in folklore. According to the legends of many lands, fairies sneak into homes and secretly exchange their otherworldly children for mortal ones. Human parents may or may not immediately realize that the fairies have substituted a "changeling" for their natural babies, but when they do the consequences can be devastating.

Some sources say the fairies use this method to get rid of inferior offspring and acquire strong, healthy babies to revitalize their own species. Other sources suggest that the fairies kidnap mortals out of curiosity or to punish humans. In some cases, the abducted infants might be sold as slaves to other spirits—a type of supernatural trafficking in children. Still other tales say that every seven years the fey were required to pay a blood sacrifice to hell. Instead of giving up their own children, they captured humans for this ancient rite; the Irish legend of Tam Lin (see Chapter 6) describes this practice.

Martin Luther, one of the human world's most prominent religious figures and leader of the Protestant Reformation, believed in changelings—and he considered them the devil's spawn. In his *Table Talk*, Luther expressed his opinion that babies with abnormalities were changelings who had no souls and were "only a piece of flesh." This view justified the neglect and cruelty toward children born with deformities—even killing helpless infants—and people who engaged in such atrocities were rarely prosecuted.

Compassion for Changelings

In her Nobel Prize–winning novel, *The Changeling*, Selma Lagerlöf addressed the centuries-old practice of abandoning and abusing children with mental or physical challenges. In the book, a female troll abducts a human baby and substitutes her own malformed child for the infant. The human father beats the changeling, but the mother intercedes and repeatedly protects the little troll. Eventually, the parents are reunited with their rightful children and the humans learn that for every hurtful act vested upon the troll baby, their own son suffered treatment in kind. Only the mortal mother's compassion saved the boy.

Mixed Marriages

Despite people's long-standing reservations about fairies, marriage between the two species often takes place in fairy tales. In some cases, the mortal disappears into the fairy realm; in other instances, the fairy chooses to live in the world of humans. Irish water spirits known as selkies and merrows often pose as humans and come on land to take human mates. According to folklore, people can trap these beautiful creatures by stealing their sealskins or red caps (respectively).

Fairies abide by strict codes of conduct, however. A human must never tell anyone that his spouse is a fairy, never see her on Saturdays, and never watch her bathe. If a mortal man hits his fairy wife, she'll leave him and return to fairyland forever. In the Welsh story "The Physicians of Myddfai," a farmer falls in love with a water fairy and they have three sons together. The boys excel at all they undertake, and when they grow up they become doctors famous for their amazing healing powers and their skill with herbal remedies—taught to them by their fairy mother. However, the fairy leaves her human mate and returns to her lake home after her husband hits her, in keeping with fairy law.

These mixed marriages can produce unusual offspring, who display the traits of both parents. However, the children may never feel truly comfortable or accepted in either realm. According to some legends, among the most famous of these mixed-blood children is the powerful sorceress Morgan Le Fey, half-sister to King Arthur.

Fairy Rings: How to Know If You're Treading on Magical Ground

If you happen to be out walking in the woods or a meadow and come upon a naturally formed circle, at least thirty or forty feet in diameter, you might have stumbled upon a fairy ring. Also known as elf rings or pixie rings, these circles may be outlined by mushrooms, or the grass might appear flattened, burned, or exceptionally green. Folklore says that fairy feet create these rings, for fairies love to gather outdoors and dance together in circles.

Whether finding a fairy ring is good luck or bad remains unclear. Our ancestors believed cattle that grazed on grass within a fairy ring would produce sour milk. Other legends warn that if you enter a fairy ring you'll contract a mysterious illness—or the fairies may force you to dance until you go mad or die. Still other tales explain that these rings serve as portals into the fairy realm, and a person who steps into such a ring will disappear into fairyland for years, maybe forever. Yet reputedly the dew that forms on fairy rings has healing properties, and some stories say if you build your home inside a fairy ring, you'll attract good luck. Supposedly, the spirits bury their treasure within these rings, and if you dig deep enough, you'll find it.

Botanists offer another theory. They suggest that a type of fungi that includes toadstools scatters its spores outward in a circular pattern. As the mushrooms grow, they use up the nitrogen in the soil, leaving a ring formation behind. This could be the origin of the connection between fairies and toadstools.

Visiting Fairyland

If you accidentally cross the line into the fairy realm, you'll likely find yourself in a time warp. What seems like an hour in their world might equal months or years in ours. Some people never return. Those who do occasionally manage to bring fairy objects back with them, such as drinking cups, coins, or good luck charms. But if you take a fairy treasure without permission, it will disappear as soon as you leave the land of the fey.

How to Win a Fairy's Favor or Avoid a Fairy's Curse

Want to attract friendly fairies? Put out food and drink for them. Many of them like milk, honey, wine, fruit, and bread. Gifts of clothing, coins, and shiny trinkets also appeal to some fairies. In return, they might offer you treasure or healing benefits. In the Brothers

Grimm's story "The Three Little Men in the Wood," fairies give a little girl gold in exchange for a bit of bread. You might try these things to win their favor too:

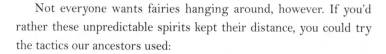

- ❖ Build a fairy house for them to live in.
- ❖ Sing and dance, and invite the fairies to join you.
- ❖ Play a flute or ring wind chimes.
- ❖ Respect nature and animals.
- ❖ Eat only organic food.
- ❖ Become vegetarian.
- ❖ Support causes that protect nature and wildlife.
- ❖ Plant a garden (no pesticides, please).

Not everyone wants fairies hanging around, however. If you'd rather these unpredictable spirits kept their distance, you could try the tactics our ancestors used:

- ❖ Display iron objects.
- ❖ Sprinkle salt around.
- ❖ Hang up garlic.
- ❖ Hang a rowan branch above your door.
- ❖ Make loud noises.
- ❖ Ring church bells.

Probably the best advice for dealing with fairies is to err on the side of caution. Let them make the first move. Be courteous, but not solicitous. Don't invite them into your life or try to insert yourself into theirs. If you meet a fairy or if one gives you a gift, keep that secret between you and the fairy. If fairies want to stop by at midnight and wash your dishes or muck out the stables, fine. But if they invite you to dinner or offer to babysit your kids, beware.

"There is never a single, orthodox version of a myth. As our circumstances change, we need to tell our stories differently in order to bring out their timeless truth."

—Karen Armstrong,
A Short History of Myth

CHAPTER 5

ℐairy ℐales

any early fairy tales were intended as morality lessons for children. They warned boys and girls to obey their parents, not talk to strangers, and so on, lest they fall victim to mischievous supernatural beings. Other stories served the same purpose for adults—especially people who believed themselves above society's laws or who thought they were clever enough to avoid punishment from the usual sources. Such tales carried simple messages, cautioning readers against greed, envy, dishonesty, laziness, etc., and threatening them with fairy retribution even if they escaped human authorities. Humans who displayed virtue, on the other hand, were often rewarded by fairies who granted wishes or proffered gifts.

Rewards for Right Living

In the Grimms' "Die Geschenke des kleinen Volkes" ("The Little Folks"), a tailor and a goldsmith traveling together happen upon a group of little people singing and dancing on a hilltop. An elderly fairy tells them to fill their pockets with lumps of coal, which magically transform into gold nuggets while the men sleep. The tailor is satisfied with this precious gift, but the greedy goldsmith wants more and returns the next night to collect as much coal as he can carry. This time, however, the coal remains coal—even his gold from the previous night turns back to coal.

Central Themes in Fairy Tales

Long before people wrote down fairy tales they passed stories along via oral tradition. Sometime around the twelfth century, people in Western Europe began recording fables, folklore, epic poems, and ballads for the educated classes. Once a story took written form, though, it became less fluid, and the author's beliefs, purpose, or interpretation influenced the direction of the story in the future.

According to Jack Zipes, editor of *The Great Fairy Tale Tradition: From Straparola and Basile to the Brothers Grimm*, the function of fairy tales is to "awaken our regard for the miraculous condition of life and to evoke profound feelings of awe and respect for life as a miraculous process, which can be altered and changed to compensate for the lack of power, wealth, and pleasure that most people experience." That's why they've endured for centuries and still fascinate us today.

Basically, all good stories—whether fairy tales or mystery novels—can be considered "heroic journeys." The protagonist/hero embarks on a quest or faces a challenge of some sort that tests and ultimately transforms him. We don't necessarily believe these stories to be factual, but still they guide, instruct, and inspire us. They give us a sense of wonder and encourage us to hope that anything can happen.

One of the intriguing aspects of fairy tales is the juxtaposition of ordinary life with an alien world—something we see not only in ancient myths but in popular movies such as *Avatar*. In fairy tales, the hero or heroine is usually a human, who finds him- or herself in an extraordinary situation with supernatural beings and must marshal every bit of personal power—including heretofore unrealized abilities—in order to succeed. Forces of good and evil confront one another and usually good triumphs. Regardless of culture or time period, fairy tales tend to follow these steps and include these plot elements:

1. The protagonist goes against a rule of society or offends a powerful person, which forces him into exile or another sort of punishment. Sometimes he desires something that his family/society/group finds unacceptable. In some cases, the protagonist crosses class barriers—social, ethnic, religious, professional, etc.—which catapults him into uncharted territory.

2. The protagonist confronts an antagonist/adversary, who more than likely is of an alien species and who poses a challenge or threat.

3. The protagonist meets an ally, who may initially seem inept or unreliable. This ally offers the hero a magical "gift" or puts him in touch with his own undeveloped gifts.

4. The protagonist encounters an obstacle or setback that forces him to rely on the gift and to trust the ally. This allows him to take on the antagonist.

5. The protagonist succeeds (finds the treasure, gets the girl, beats the opponent, etc.) by persevering, believing in miracles, and tapping his formerly unacknowledged abilities.

Categorizing Fairy Tales

Similar themes appear in fairy tales from around the world. In order to examine the evolution of stories, folklorists developed a system called the Aarne-Thompson Folktale Types and Motif Index that groups stories according to dominant motifs. Originated by Antti Aarne in 1910 (and refined many times since), the index organizes stories into general classifications, such as animal tales, fairy tales, and so on. Then it breaks down those classifications further, based on more specific details.

Tales of magic, for instance, are assigned numbers 300–745. Within that category, we find subcategories for stories that involve supernatural adversaries (300–399), supernatural or enchanted relatives (400–459), supernatural helpers (500–559), magical items (560–649), supernatural power or knowledge (650–699), and more.

The Aarne-Thompson Index covers more than 2,500 plot elements that storytellers have used for centuries as structures for their yarn-spinning. It also lets folklorists see how stories get handed down through generations and passed from one culture to another. By studying themes in fairy tales, researchers can understand such things as behavior and ethics in various parts of the world, migrations of people from one country to another, and changing societal norms over time.

Why Do We Call Them Fairy Tales?

Not all fairy tales concern fairies. Once upon a time, these engaging stories were called "wonder tales." In the seventeenth century, French writers began taking old folktales and reworking them into literary forms for elite, sophisticated readers. Some of our favorite stories come from that period, including "Cinderella" and "Sleeping Beauty." The French referred to them as *conte de fées*, which translates into English as "fairy tale."

Mores, Ideals, and Prejudice in Fairy Tales

Throughout the ages, fairy tales have served as vehicles for conveying social ideas and ethics. In some instances, they also offered commentary on historic events. Many of our best-known stories have evolved over time, with each author or collector adapting the tales to his or her culture, era, and even personal biases.

Seventeenth-century French author Charles Perrault might be thought of as an entertaining Emily Post of the period. His fairy tales served as guides in etiquette and conduct for the young ladies of King Louis XIV's court. In the nineteenth century, the Brothers Grimm collected older stories and revised them to socialize lower-class German children and teach them how to behave. The Grimms, coming from the academic class, took an elitist view, and their stories present a perspective that today we'd consider sexist and racist—the Third Reich even used some of these fairy tales as propaganda.

Before the twentieth century, fairy tales were much darker and more violent than the ones we enjoy today. Modern adaptations excise the more gruesome bits to make them palatable for young readers (and their parents). For example, in the Grimms' version of "Cinderella" the mean stepsisters cut off parts of their feet to try to squeeze into Cinderella's tiny glass slipper—a feature nicely omitted in Disney's retelling. In Hans Christian Andersen's story "The Little Mermaid," the heroine has her tongue cut out, loses her exquisite voice, and suffers terrible pain each time she takes a step—and her beloved prince ends up marrying another woman. How many modern girls would find that tale entertaining?

Today's fairy tales show a prettier picture, but like their predecessors, they still reflect moral messages and our present-day attitudes—that's their underlying purpose. *The Children's Book of Virtues*, edited by William J. Bennett and published in 1995, intentionally compiles fairy tales and other children's stories "to help parents introduce to their children the essentials of good character."

Fantasy fiction has taken over the darker side of fairy tales. In these stories, good and bad become blurred—the heroes have flaws and the villains aren't unrelentingly evil. The characters still portray qualities we admire—courage, loyalty, honesty, generosity—but the element of ambiguity provides greater intrigue and believability. As in real life, we don't always know how the story will turn out.

Testing for Morality

In the fall of 2009 and spring of 2010, a group of researchers at the College of Charleston, South Carolina, conducted a study of undergraduates to investigate whether fantasy role-playing games influenced positive or negative moral development in young people. They also wanted to find out if game-play might extend the participants' ability to make moral decisions beyond their ordinary range of experience. At the end of the study, the researchers concluded that "imaginative role-playing games can be effective for fostering moral growth."

Psychology's Take on Fairy Tales

Freud, Jung, and other psychoanalysts used fairy tales as a tool for understanding the human psyche. Freud believed that fairy tales served as portals into the unconscious. He also thought they contained wish-fulfillment and sexual themes. Jung, who wrote extensively about archetypes in what he called "the collective unconscious," saw these archetypes abounding in fairy tales, and he used fairy tales to

analyze patients' dreams. Some Jungian therapists suggest that the various characters in fairy tales represent different aspects of the individual—we all have the hero and the villain, the trickster and the mage, in us.

Psychology also looks at the characters and situations presented in fairy tales as symbols. In *The Wizard of Oz*, the flying monkeys represent fear. The forest in "Hansel and Gretel" indicates the confusion and sense of being lost that we all feel from time to time. In "Beauty and the Beast," the beast symbolizes the inner darkness inside each of us that keeps us and others from seeing our goodness. The fairy tale "fool" (a character who seems childish, handicapped, stupid, or inept in some way) signifies the part of ourselves that we haven't acknowledged.

Fairy tales can offer guidance for solving human dilemmas, too. Often they depict, symbolically, the struggles we face in our daily lives. They teach us to persevere against seemingly impossible odds, to set aside our egos and ally ourselves with others in order to prevail, and to be true to ourselves in the face of opposition. Psychologist Bruno Bettelheim, author of the mid-1970s book *The Uses of Enchantment: The Meaning and Importance of Fairy Tales*, proposed that fairy tales help children to cope in a world where they have little power and adults rule.

Like dreams, fairy tales give us a way to see ourselves, our motivations, and the hidden parts of ourselves more clearly. They also show us the world in which we live, what it expects of us, and how to navigate its waters safely.

Fairies at the Movies

Although many movies have featured the fey folk, two from the 1980s stand out:

THE DARK CRYSTAL AND LABYRINTH

Jim Henson and Frank Oz of Muppet fame directed *The Dark Crystal* (1982), and Brian Froud, author and illustrator of such books as *Trolls* and *World of Fairie*, created the concept art. The story centers on the evolution and conflict of two species: the reptilian Skeksis and the Mystics. The story is a race to find the crystal shard that can restore oneness to the world and prevent the Skeksis from ruling the land forever. Jim Henson voiced the lead character, an elflike creature named Jen, who embarks on this heroic quest. Although some critics considered the story derivative and simplistic, most agreed that the special effects and the way in which Henson voiced the character of Jen were exceptional.

Henson, Oz, and Froud came together again in 1986 for *Labyrinth*, starring David Bowie and Jennifer Connolly. Monty Python's Terry Jones wrote the first draft of the script, making it weirder than *The Dark Crystal*, but also lighter and more humorous than the first film. In the story, the goblin king (Bowie) captures a young girl's baby brother and she must travel through an elaborate labyrinth to find him.

Other contributors to the film's final screenplay included Elaine May and George Lucas.

HARVEY

Among the most enduring and magical of classic American movies is the 1950 feature *Harvey*, starring Jimmy Stewart. The movie, adapted from a play by Mary Chase, tells the story of Elwood P. Dowd, a charming, apparently lackadaisical and slightly alcoholic man whose constant companion and best friend is an invisible six-foot-three-and-a-half-inch-tall rabbit named—you guessed it!—Harvey.

The film is a tribute to the power of imagination. Although Elwood's obsession with Harvey drives his sister and her daughter up a wall, it rarely occurs to them to doubt the rabbit's existence. When they attempt to have Elwood confined to a sanitarium, the doctor in charge of the hospital comes to not only accept Harvey but to need his assistance in recapturing a simpler time in his life.

What is Harvey, exactly? In the film, Elwood explains to an interested companion that Harvey is a pooka—a magical fairy who can stop time:

> *"Harvey can look at your clock and stop it. And you can go anywhere you like—with anyone you like—and stay as long as you like. And when you get back, not one minute will have ticked by . . . You see, science has overcome time and space. Well, Harvey has overcome not only time and space—but any objections."*

Like all pookas, Harvey has a mischievous side (at one point in the movie, when one of the characters looks up the definition of "pooka" in the dictionary, Harvey uses the definition to say hello to him).

Of course, the story ends as all good fairy stories do, with Elwood and his pooka friend contentedly wandering, arm in arm, toward a glowing sunset.

PART TWO

Fairies from Around the World

"Stories, like people and butterflies and songbirds' eggs and human hearts and dreams, are also fragile things, made up of nothing stronger or more lasting than twenty-six letters and a handful of punctuation marks. Or they are words on the air, composed of sounds and ideas—abstract, invisible, gone once they've been spoken—and what could be more frail than that? But some stories, small, simple ones about setting out on adventures or people doing wonders, tales of miracles and monsters, have outlasted all the people who told them, and some of them have outlasted the lands in which they were created."

—Neil Gaiman, *Fragile Things*

"In oldè dayès of the king
    Artoúr,

Of which that Bretons speken
    gret honoúr,

All was this lond fulfilled of
    faerie;

The Elf-quene with her joly
    compagnie,

Danced ful oft in many a grenè
    mede."

—Geoffrey Chaucer, *The Canterbury Tales*

CHAPTER 6

Fairies of the British Isles

s Chaucer's Wife of Bath explains, fairies once inhabited the countryside and woodlands of England, Scotland, and Wales in great numbers. But by the time Percy Bysshe Shelley wrote his mystical poem about the fairy Queen Mab, the fey had started leaving England. Industry, technology, and urban expansion had taken over their territory, and rational minds no longer believed in such silliness as fairies. Yet, people clung to the idea that elves, gnomes, sprites, and otherworldly beings still lived among humans—some even reported seeing these creatures around rural Britain. Today, despite the continued growth of technology and materialism, fairies are making a comeback of unprecedented proportion.

The Seelie and Unseelie Courts

Scottish mythology refers to two groups of fairies, known as the Seelie and the Unseelie courts. Legends describe the Seelie—the "blessed," "holy," or "light" fey—as good spirits who sometimes come to the aid of humans. At one time, the Seelie interacted with mortals and rewarded people who helped them, but your chances of seeing them today are slim. These beautiful and fun-loving fairies enjoy music, games, poetry, and riddles. Linked with the forces of regeneration, they travel on the winds and live in a land filled with sunshine and laughter. Like all fairies, they're unpredictable and play tricks on people, but they intend no serious harm.

A Compassionate Fairy Queen

Once upon a time, a Scottish knight offended a woman who possessed magical powers. The angry lass turned him into a hideous half-reptilian creature and left him lying, cold and hungry, beneath a tree for months. On Samhain Eve (October 31), the miserable enchanted knight heard music coming toward him and saw the Seelie Court parading through the countryside. The Seelie Queen spotted the lizard-man and took pity on him, letting him lay his head in her lap while she stroked his scaly form throughout the night. In the morning, the reptile skin split open, freeing the knight from the evil spell.

The Unseelie Court—the "unholy" or "dark" fey—consists of a bunch of bad guys bent on tormenting humans. They strike first, without provocation, showing up after dark and beating their unwary victims just for sport. They also kidnap people and keep them as pets or servants, forcing them to live in the fairies' dark, unhappy land. The Unseelie symbolize the forces of death and appear as a black cloud in the sky—although you can't actually see the fairies themselves. But if you hear the Unseelie howling or cackling on the wind, run!

The Unseelie's Revenge

Long ago, the Unseelie's aggressive and fierce nature saved all the fairies from extinction. An evil wizard, a human determined to destroy the fey, summoned horrible demons who attacked the fairies. However, the Unseelie fought with such ferociousness that they eventually beat back the demons. Although the Unseelie troops sustained severe injuries, their bravery enabled the other fairies to escape. To this day, the Unseelie hate mortals and assault them in retribution for the violence a human perpetrated on the fey.

Tam Lin

Before people began writing down stories, Scottish bards told a darkly beautiful ballad about a young knight named Tam Lin who falls into the fairies' clutches. The ancient tale continues to inspire modern writers and musicians, including Holly Black and the folk-rock band Fairport Convention.

Captured by the fairy queen when he falls from his horse, Tam Lin is a handsome chap who lives at Carterhaugh and demands a toll from all who enter there—for young women, the fee is gold, their mantles of green, or their maidenheads. Thus Janet, the tale's heroine, is forbidden by her father to go there, even though she owns the place.

The independent young woman refuses to be curtailed by either her father or the resident rogue and goes to the forest near Carterhaugh. There she picks a double rose from a bush, which triggers Tam Lin's appearance. He insists on his fee: Janet's virginity. But this isn't a case of ordinary rape; it's enchantment, and Janet falls in love with the mysterious fellow. Janet becomes pregnant but refuses to reveal the name of her lover. She returns to Carterhaugh to tell Tam Lin he's going to be a father and to learn whether any human blood runs in his veins.

He admits he was once mortal but has lived a long time in fairyland and the queen favors him as her best knight. He also tells Janet that every seven years the fairies must tithe one of their own to hell so that the others may thrive. This year on Halloween, as he rides in a procession with other knights, he fears he'll become the sacrificial victim. He implores Janet to pull him from his white horse and rescue him from the fairies.

> *"And pleasant is the fairy-land,*
> *But, an eerie tale to tell,*
> *Ay at the end of seven years,*
> *We pay a tiend to hell,*
> *I am sae fair and fu o flesh,*
> *I'm feard it be mysel."*

—Robert Burns

That night, when Janet does as he asks, the angry fairy queen tries to force Janet to release her lover by turning him into a series of frightening things: a newt, a snake, a lion, a hot coal. By refusing to fall for the queen's tricks, however, the mortal bests the fairy and saves her lover.

This transformation tale shows that fairies have long been known to change themselves and humans into other creatures by magical means. By holding fast and fearing not, the story tells us, we can transcend the demons and trials we encounter in life. "Tam Lin" is also about feminine power, referencing the pre-Christian matriarchal times. The male knight is first captured by the fairy queen, then must rely on his lover to rescue him from fairyland.

The Tylwyth Teg

In 1188, the Archbishop Baldwin and his companion Giraldus Cambrensis (Gerald of Wales) traveled through Wales trying to drum up interest in the forthcoming Crusades. Giraldus kept a journal along the way—the oldest written account of Welsh fey, called the *Itinerary of Giraldus Cambrensis*—in which he mentions a beautiful race of supernatural beings about three feet tall known as the Tylwyth Teg. Also called the gwyllion or ellyllon, these fairies abide in a hidden land called Annwn, or the Otherworld. To reach their home, they must slip through secret passageways in lakes, rivers, or other bodies of water.

The Tylwyth Teg love flowers and gardening, and Annwn blossoms with all sorts of amazing flora, fauna, and fruit-bearing trees. Each year on Beltane (May 1), according to legend, the fairies used to hold an open house and invited visitors to come to their magnificent homeland. Guests entered a doorway in a rock near a lake in

Brecknock that led to an island in the lake's center. There the Tylwyth Teg entertained the lucky guests with music and fed them the luscious fruit grown on the island. But the fairies stipulated that no one could take anything away from the island and its location must remain secret. One man, however, failed to heed the fairies' request and stole a flower. The Tylwyth Teg closed the door to Annwn forever and never again invited outsiders to their enchanting home.

Some sources say the fairies live in clans—the name Tylwyth Teg translates as "fair family"—presided over by the eldest male and the eldest female. When the children reach maturity at about age 100, they move away and live with their peers until they marry, in much the same way as human youth do.

Usually friendly to mortals, the female fairies sometimes marry human men. They also interbreed with other types of fairies, producing elfin offspring known as Bendith y Mamau. The Tylwyth Teg are said to be extremely fond of handsome mortal male children, especially blonds, and abduct them if they get the chance. For this reason, wary Welsh parents once attired their sons in dresses until the age of six so the fairies would mistake them for girls and leave them alone.

The Welsh Water Horse

Welsh folklore tells of a dangerous enchanted horse called a ceffyl dwr that lives in the water. It lets human riders mount it but then throws them off, which usually results in their deaths. Supposedly, though, religious leaders can safely ride the water horse—but they must remain silent if they want to stay in the saddle.

Morgan Le Fey

The court of King Arthur provides the setting for Britain's best-loved and most enduring legend. Among the most fascinating characters in the Arthurian tales is the king's half-sister, Morgan Le Fey. Beautiful, powerful, and enigmatic, Morgan is often portrayed as an evil sorceress, the bad girl on the block, and a force to be reckoned with. Nobody really knows the truth about Morgan—the legends have been told by so many people over so many years that it's impossible to know which, if any, version has veracity. Pretty much everyone, though, agrees that this enchanting creature was half-human and half-fairy.

Geoffrey of Monmouth first mentioned Morgan in the mid-twelfth century, in his *Vita Merlini*. According to Geoffrey, she could fly and change her shape at will. And, like many fairies, she had extraordinary healing powers. She made her home on the magical Isle of Avalon, which some researchers link with the modern-day city of Glastonbury in England.

A couple decades later, the French poet Chrétien de Troyes established Morgan as Arthur's half-sister, a bastard child sent to a nunnery where she learned reading, writing, astrology, and healing. The great magician Merlin taught her the art of magic. Supposedly, Merlin loved Morgan, but she only wanted his knowledge, not the mage himself.

Instead, the legends say, Morgan loved Arthur's friend Lancelot, but Lancelot only had eyes for Arthur's wife, Guinevere. Not surprisingly, Morgan hated her sister-in-law, the queen. Other French writers proposed that Morgan hated both Guinevere and Arthur for breaking up her love affair with the queen's cousin Guiomar. Yet, Morgan shows compassion for her half-brother when she ferries him away from his last battle, fatally wounded, to the mystical Isle of Avalon.

Sir Thomas Malory—a mysterious British figure in his own right, whose exact identity and heritage remain uncertain—penned another notable interpretation of the Arthurian legend in his fifteenth-century work *Le Morte d'Arthur*. Malory paints Morgan as an adulteress, a malcontent, a disruptive force in Arthur's court, and a magician who could summon the dead. At a time when the Catholic Church's influence in England was starting to come into question, Malory depicts the fairy as a subversive symbol of the political machinations of the period, a counterpoint to the Church's teachings.

During the late nineteenth and early twentieth centuries, Morgan got a lot of bad press from numerous writers—not that she'd ever been depicted kindly. Perhaps the idea of a powerful, intelligent, overtly sexual female who also possessed occult knowledge was too much for Britain's straight-laced Victorian readers. But in the late twentieth

and early twenty-first centuries, Morgan received better treatment as women's political and social positions advanced in the West. Author Marion Zimmer Bradley's *The Mists of Avalon*—published during a time of pagan resurgence in modern-day England and the United States—portrays Morgan as a representative of the Old Religion that predated Christianity's ascension into Britain.

An odd blend of magical fairy abilities and human emotions, Morgan Le Fey is a complicated character. Like other fairies, and other fairy tales, this legend's evolution cleverly reveals almost a millennium's worth of changing ideas about women, religion, and power. Through Morgan, we can trace the evolution of women in the English-speaking world since the Middle Ages.

Fairy Helpers

Need a little help around the house or yard? Invite Britain's brownies to lend a hand. These benevolent little fellows, usually about three feet tall, show up at night to do chores for household members. They tidy up the kitchen, mow the grass, run errands, and make themselves useful in dozens of ways. These unassuming fairy folk wear ragged brown servants' clothing and sport shaggy hair and beards. It's not a good idea to try to give them better garments, though, for they may take offense and leave.

Shakespeare's Fairies

Fairies became fashionable in English literature during the sixteenth century, due in part to William Shakespeare's delightful romantic comedy *A Midsummer Night's Dream.* In the play, three fairies—King Oberon, his lovely queen Titania, and the king's servant Puck (a.k.a. Robin Goodfellow)—meet with a group of Greek nobles and Athenian craftsmen. After a disagreement between Oberon and Titania over a changeling child she adores, the queen refuses to sleep with her husband, so he sends the fun-loving prankster, Puck, to procure a magic flower. Oberon plans to play a trick on Titania by spreading the flower's juice on the sleeping queen's eyelids, which will cause her to fall in love with whatever creature she sees when she first opens her eyes. While she's blinded by love, the jealous fairy king hopes to nab the little boy.

Oberon also tells Puck to anoint the eyes of one of the Greek men so he'll desire a woman who loves him and whom he's treated unkindly. But Puck makes a mistake—and that's when the fun begins. During the enchanted night, all sorts of mischief, magic, and mix-ups happen deep in the forest. All ends well, however, for the Bard's fun-loving fairies never mean any real harm.

"Over hill, over dale,
Thorough bush, thorough brier,
Over park, over pale,
Thorough flood, thorough fire,
I do wander everywhere,
Swifter than the moon's sphere;
And I serve the fairy queen,
To dew her orbs upon the green."

—William Shakespeare, *A Midsummer Night's Dream*

Shakespeare seemed versed in fairy folklore and found the fey intriguing literary subjects, because he also wrote about them in *The Tempest*, *Romeo and Juliet*, and *The Merry Wives of Windsor*. Usually he painted them as diminutive, beautiful, and capricious. In *A Midsummer*

Night's Dream, Puck explains that when Oberon and Titania argue, " . . . all their elves for fear/Creep into acorn cups, and hide them there." In *The Tempest,* the spirit Ariel displays other fairy traits: He's mischievous, of course; he can travel about instantaneously; and he can shapeshift.

Most likely, Shakespeare was familiar with the epic poem *The Faerie Queene* by Edmund Spenser, first published in 1590, six years before the Bard completed *A Midsummer Night's Dream.* In the allegorical four-book series—Spenser's longest and most important work—the poet uses Queen Elizabeth I as a model for Gloriana, the queen of the fairies. Apparently, Elizabeth liked the comparison, for she bestowed the honor of poet laureate on Spenser.

Painting Shakespeare's Fairies

Shakespeare's fairies provided inspiration for English artists from the eighteenth to the twentieth centuries, including J.M.W. Turner, Sir Joseph Noel Pato, Richard Dadd, Arthur Rackham, and William Blake. During the sexually repressive Victorian era, fairies, like mermaids, served as sensual subjects for artists and collectors alike— mythological females could appear nude or wearing diaphanous garments, unlike mortal ladies of the time.

Queen Mab

Although Shakespeare named the Queen of the Fairies Titania in *A Midsummer Night's Dream*, he calls her Queen Mab in *Romeo and Juliet*. The Bard describes Mab as "In shape no bigger than an agate stone/ On the fore-finger of an alderman" and says she flies into people's nostrils while they sleep, then enters their brains, where she inspires dreams. She likes to play tricks on humans, too; one of her favorite pranks is braiding the manes and tails of horses. Bad luck befell anyone who tried to undo the braids. (See Chapter 3 for a modern-day account of this practice.)

Percy Bysshe Shelley, in his mythic poem "Queen Mab" (1813) treated the fairy queen more lovingly, describing her as "wondrous and the beautiful / So bright, so fair, so wild a shape." According to Shelley, she drives a pearl chariot, holds a magic wand, and speaks in dulcet tones. Queen Mab has a lot of responsibilities, too. She commands the stars and the oceans, keeps the world's secrets, and teaches what the future holds. She lives on a golden island in a silver sea, in a palace with a sky-blue dome and floors made of light, where time and space lack all meaning. From here, she oversees human activities, past, present, and future.

Like other fairies, Mab is a nature lover. To the soul of a woman named Ianthe, whom the queen takes to heaven for a fantastic journey before returning the mortal to earth, Mab says:

> *"Look on yonder earth:*
> *The golden harvests spring; the unfailing sun*
> *Sheds light and life; the fruits, the flowers, the trees,*
> *Arise in due succession; all things speak*
> *Peace, harmony and love. The universe,*
> *In Nature's silent eloquence, declares*
> *That all fulfil the works of love and joy."*

Some authors depict the fairy queen in a positive light, granting wishes for humans as she does in J.M. Barrie's *The Little White Bird*, when she gives Peter Pan his ability to fly. Others paint her as scheming, dangerous, and unsympathetic to humans. American writer Jim Butcher, in the *Dresden Files* series, portrays Mab as an attractive white-haired woman, the Queen of Air and Darkness, a powerful fairy queen of the Unseelie Court, cold-hearted, with a nasty temper. In Simon R. Green's *Secret History* series she's a usurper to the throne of Oberon and Titania.

Perhaps the complex Queen Mab appeals to writers and readers because, like so many fairies, she combines the qualities of light and dark. She's an enigma who doesn't think, act, or feel things the way humans do, which keeps us guessing as to what she'll do next.

Fairy Sightings

English poet and artist William Blake claimed to have seen a fairy funeral in his garden. Allan Cunningham, in his book *The Lives of the Most Eminent British Painters, Sculptors, and Architects,* quoted Blake as saying he observed "a procession of creatures of the size and colour of green and grey grasshoppers, bearing a body laid out on a rose-leaf, which they buried with songs, and then disappeared." Fairies live a very long time, but apparently they aren't immortal.

Collecting Fairies

We have Scottish writer, anthropologist, and historian Andrew Lang to thank for collecting and preserving fairy tales from many lands through the ages. Lang compiled the stories in a series of anthologies, organized by colors: *The Blue Fairy Book*, *The Yellow Fairy Book*, and so on. His collections offered the first English-language translations of some of these tales, which originated in Africa, China, India, Russia, and other parts of the world. Lang's fairy tale series contained twelve volumes, published between 1889 and 1910. He also wrote his own fairy tales as well as numerous fiction and nonfiction works.

Gilbert and Sullivan's *Iolanthe*

Three centuries after Shakespeare wrote *A Midsummer Night's Dream*, the creative team of W.S. Gilbert and Arthur Sullivan brought fairies and humans together for a romantic romp in the political satire *Iolanthe*. Iolanthe, a fairy, does what fairies sometimes do, but shouldn't: She marries a mortal and gives birth to a mixed-blood child named Strephon. Her mistake gets her exiled from the land of the fey and she raises her son as a lowly shepherd. The half-man, half-fairy falls in love with a shepherdess named Phyllis and plans to marry her—but it turns out the entire House of Lords and the Lord Chancellor in particular also adore Phyllis.

The complications don't end there, however. Phyllis sees Strephon and his mother, Iolanthe, together and believes he's cheating on her—fairies don't age, so the shepherdess thinks she has a youthful rival. She decides to dump Strephon and marry a lord, which angers the fairies. As retribution, the fey send Strephon to Parliament and cast a spell that makes the peers pass all Strephon's bills—including one that requires Parliament's seats to be filled based on intelligence rather than birth. In the end, Strephon and Phyllis get back together. The other fairies marry the lords and take them to fairyland, which allows intelligent people to take over the House of Lords, and everyone lives happily ever after.

Okay, a totally ridiculous plot, but such fun that the original operetta ran 398 performances. More than 100 years later, *Iolanthe* continues to delight audiences on both sides of the Atlantic.

> "O, hark, O, hear! how thin and clear
> And thinner, clearer, farther going!
> O, sweet and far from cliff and scar
> The horns of Elfland faintly blowing!
> Blow, let us hear the purple glens replying,
> Blow, bugle ; answer, echoes, dying, dying, dying."
>
> —Alfred Lord Tennyson

Tinker Bell: The Most Famous Fairy of All

We owe our modern-day concept of fairies to Scottish author J.M. Barrie, whose 1904 play *Peter Pan; or, the Boy Who Wouldn't Grow Up* introduced the character we know and love as Tinker Bell. But in Barrie's original production, she only played a small role as a common kitchen fairy, not even worthy of having an actress to portray her—she appeared merely as a circle of light. To bring her onstage, a person held a mirror to reflect lamplight while another tinkled bells to represent her voice. (Apparently only other fairies could understand what she said.) This theatrical representation of Tinker Bell continued into the mid-1950s, when the musical version starring Mary Martin played on Broadway.

In true fairy tale fashion, Barrie continued to revise and update the play in later productions, and in 1911, he published a book version titled *Peter and Wendy*. Almost a century later, Tink and her pals showed up again in the official sequel, *Peter Pan in Scarlet*, by Geraldine McCaughrean.

Tinker Bell has Walt Disney to thank for making her what she is today. Disney loved *Peter Pan* and in 1935 he began adapting the story as an animated feature film. Like fairy tale creators before him, he and his staff rewrote the original play numerous times, altering the plot and characters. Early versions contained darker scenes and plot elements that ended up on the cutting room floor. The movie was temporarily tabled during World War II, but in 1953, RKO Pictures released the movie that captured the hearts of millions of viewers.

"Fairies have to be one thing or the other, because being so small they unfortunately have room for one feeling only at a time."

— J.M. Barrie, *Peter Pan*

As often happens with contemporary revisions of older fairy tales, Disney cleaned up Barrie's story, and in so doing he tamed the tempestuous Tink. Disney's animated film portrays Tinker Bell as jealous and volatile, but in Barrie's tale she's downright dangerous. For example, a vindictive Tink convinces one of Peter Pan's comrades, known as the Lost Boys, to shoot Wendy in the heart and then make it seem as if Peter ordered her death. Barrie also portrays Tinker Bell as voluptuous and sexy, passionately in love with Peter, and more mature than the other characters. She can't really rival Wendy as Peter's love interest, however, because she's too small. The triangle between Tinker Bell, Peter, and Wendy in Barrie's story presents the theme of budding sexuality in the boy and girl, something the animated film downplays.

Tinker Bell must have worked her magic to wrangle herself a bigger piece of the action than Barrie originally gave her, for today she's the most famous fairy of all time.

Fooled by "Fairies"

In 1920, people around the world—including Sir Arthur Conan Doyle, author of the Sherlock Holmes mysteries—believed they saw living proof that fairies actually existed. A series of photographs snapped by two cousins, Elsie Wright and Frances Griffiths, showed the girls playing with dainty, winged beings in a Cottingley garden. When Elsie's mother took the photos to Edward Gardner, a leading figure in the Theosophical movement who pronounced them legitimate, the images began making their way around Britain's Spiritualist community. Not until 1981 did Elsie Wright admit to the hoax: The fairies were really just paper cutouts.

Beyond the Fields We Know

Among the most important literary influences on twentieth-century fantasy writers was the Irish writer Edward John Moreton Drax Plunkett, Eighteenth Baron of Dunsany. A member of the gradually decaying Irish nobility, he divided his youth between Ireland and England, where he absorbed the various fairy traditions of both countries.

An extensive revival of interest in Irish literature and legends occurred during the early part of the twentieth century. This renaissance stimulated such authors as W.B. Yeats, John Millington Synge, and the dramatists Lady Gregory and Sean O'Casey. It also deeply influenced Dunsany, who found the rich folkloric traditions of his native Ireland fascinating. Several of his novels reflect this, including *Don Rodriguez: Chronicles of Shadow Valley*, *The Charwoman's Shadow*, and *The King of Elfland's Daughter*, as do his numerous short story collections with such titles as *At the Edge of the World* and *Beyond the Fields We Know*.

The Revival of Fantasy

Few modern readers (other than literary scholars) knew anything of Dunsany's works until the 1970s when Ballantine Press began publishing classic fantasies and fairy tales under the imprint "Ballantine Adult Fantasy" series. The series eventually contained more than 100 titles and included such classic fantasy authors as William Morris, William Hope Hodgson, L. Sprague de Camp, James Branch Cabell, and Mervyn Peake. The series served as an important introduction to fantasy for many writers who came of age in the 1970s and 1980s.

The King of Elfland's Daughter is probably the best known of Dunsany's novels. In it, a mortal land, Erl, decides it wants to be ruled by a fairy princess, so the king's son goes to Elfland to fetch back the ruler's daughter to be his bride. The marriage doesn't work out initially—the elfin bride is bored and feels out of place in the mortal realm—and eventually she flees back to Elfland. Her husband has no choice but to pursue her into the realm of Fairie. After many adventures, the two reunite and the King of Fairie's powerful magic draws Erl into Elfland.

C.S. Lewis and the Creatures of Narnia

During the 1930s, 1940s, and 1950s, a group of Oxford friends met regularly in the Bird and Baby pub to drink, relax, and read manuscripts to one another of fictional works they were writing in their spare time. Regulars of the group included Oxford don J.R.R. Tolkien, the poet and fantasist Charles Williams, and the writer C.S. Lewis. The group called themselves the Inklings.

Lewis, whose primary interests were more theological and philosophical than literary, was described by his friends as having a "boyish" element in his personality. Perhaps that's why his stories are more lighthearted than those of his friend Tolkien. In 1950, Lewis published *The Lion, the Witch, and the Wardrobe*, the first of seven books about the magical land of Narnia, a place inhabited by fantastic creatures such as dryads, dwarfs, centaurs, giants, and talking animals.

The mighty lion Aslan ruled the land, although he was away from it most of the time ("After all, it's not as if he were a *tame* lion!"). *The Lion, the Witch, and the Wardrobe* tells the story of four English girls and boys who found a way to get from our world into Narnia and became mighty kings and queens of the land.

Magical creatures abound in Narnia. In *The Voyage of the Dawn Treader*, three human children take a fantastic voyage through the seas around Narnia. Among other wonders, they meet little people who live under the sea and who ride seahorses and hold court beneath the waves. In *The Silver Chair*, two children embark on a dangerous mission to rescue an imprisoned prince. During their quest they receive aid from a curious creature called a marsh-wiggle—tall, muddy-looking, solemn, and deeply pessimistic in outlook. They also encounter dwarfs who live not merely beneath the earth but actually down inside its deepest chasms, caves lit by many-colored fires where living gems can be plucked by adventurous souls.

As a dedicated member of the Church of England, Lewis wanted to spread the message of Christianity, and he made his stories allegories of the Christian church and faith. But we can also read them as exciting adventure stories that continue to enchant and excite us.

The Mouse That Talked

Though not precisely a fairy, one of the most endearing characters in the Narnia stories is Reepicheep the talking mouse. He stands about three feet tall with dark, almost-black fur and wears a thin scarlet headband with a feather tucked in it. He carries a glittering sword, which prepares him to avenge his—or anyone else's—honor at a moment's notice.

J.R.R. Tolkien and the Hobbits

"In a hole in the ground there lived a hobbit." Professor John Ronald Reuel Tolkien, seized by a moment of inspiration, jotted down that sentence while grading papers at Oxford University nearly a century ago. So began a legacy of fairy fantasy literature that continues to captivate us today. Although Britain's folklore offered a wealth of material for novelists, J.R.R. Tolkien drew on ancient European mythology and Germanic/Norse legends for his award-winning book, *The Hobbit*, published in 1937, and the subsequent *Lord of the Rings* trilogy.

In addition to the furry-footed, pint-size, hole-dwelling, humanoid creatures he called hobbits, Tolkien populated his magical Middle-earth with trolls, elves, dwarfs, wizards, goblins, even talking trees. He portrayed elves as handsome beings with melodic voices and great skill as craftsmen. His dwarfs, however, were greedy and unreliable, his trolls short-tempered and stupid. Goblins, of course, exemplified evil.

Among the world's best-loved books, Tolkien's tales have sold in the tens of millions. Within a year of the release of the movie versions of *The Fellowship of the Ring* (2001) and *The Two Towers* (2002), the two films had raked in more than $1 billion at the box office internationally and won six Oscars; the third in the series, *Return of the King*, was one of the highest grossing movies of all time. A new three-film series, *The Hobbit*, directed by Peter Jackson and starring Martin Freeman, with opening dates in 2012, 2013, and 2014, give fans another opportunity to enjoy Tolkien's enduring adventures.

Neil Gaiman's Fairy Nuala

"Fairy tales are more than true: not because they tell us that dragons exist, but because they tell us that dragons can be beaten," author Neil Gaiman explains. Gaiman, one of this century's most popular fairy tale writers, brings readers into the complex Faerie world and its inhabitants in his *Sandman* series and other works.

Nuala, for instance, displays many of the traits and behaviors typical of fairies. A rather ordinary-looking pixie, she puts on her magic glamour to transform herself into a gorgeous blonde. This shapeshifter moves back and forth between the human world and the realm of Faerie, governed by the fairy queen Titania, and she gets involved with mortal men.

Nuala lacks the power and mystique of some literary fairies, such as Morgan Le Fey and Queen Mab, and she seems willing to succumb to others (males in particular) because of her attraction to Morpheus and her devotion to her brother, which may represent a male fantasy of controlling and disempowering females. Her character grows through her sense of duty, perhaps hinting at Christian morality themes found in some older fairy tales. However, Nuala is hardly weak. Rather, she shows her strength of will and courage when she chooses to relinquish her magical glamour and face the world as she truly is.

Caroline Luzzatto, writing for *The Virginian-Pilot*, puts her finger on the source of Gaiman's appeal—and the appeal of fairy tales in general: "They resonate because they target universal fears and longings, and Gaiman has a way of making bogeymen feel real, filling in the details of their wardrobe and vocabulary and sour breath, hinting at what the monsters themselves are afraid of, and probing, perhaps, who the world's real monsters might be."

"There is a latent fairy in all women, but look how carefully we have to secrete her in order to be taken seriously. And fairies come in all shapes, colours, sizes and types, they don't have to be fluffy. They can be demanding and furious if they like. They do, however, have to wear a tiara. That much is compulsory."

— Dawn French, *A Tiny Bit Marvellous*

The Gentleman with Thistle-Down Hair

"It's a sort of symbiotic thing, the relationship between magicians and fairies, which is that they build up magic," says Susanna Clarke, author of the alternate history novel *Jonathan Strange and Mr. Norrell*. "The relationship between the two races has formed English magic."

Revisiting this relationship is at the heart of Clarke's highly acclaimed novel, published in 2004. In it, she introduces two nineteenth-century magicians who seek to bring magic back to an England that's become too industrialized, and an intriguing antagonist, known only as The Gentleman with Thistle-Down Hair, a moniker that refers to his most striking trait: his shock of white hair. The Gentleman, who's the fairy ruler of the kingdom of Lost Hope, doesn't reveal his real name because if you're a spirit and a magician knows your name, he has power over you—and the Gentleman has no intention of handing over power to his enemies.

The Gentleman bears no resemblance to the tiny gossamer-winged creatures who flit among the flowers. He stands a little taller than an average man and has no wings—and he's certainly not benevolent. In addition to his stunning white hair, the handsome Gentleman's features reflect a Germanic/Scandinavian heritage: pale skin, blue eyes, angular features. But he also has curiously upturned dark eyebrows, and his skin feels icy cold to the touch. Like many fairies, though, he apparently prefers the color green, for he wears a green waistcoat cut in the height of fashion (for the Regency era, anyway). He also exhibits some typical fairy behavior—he's in sync with the forces of nature, he can shapeshift, he's capricious, he likes to kidnap people, and he can foretell the future, which he does by viewing the entrails of dying soldiers. The Gentleman shows little concern for the feelings or well-being of humans and abides by his own code, which includes casting dastardly spells on some of the other characters in the novel. In *Salon* magazine, writer Laura Miller called the "muddy, bloody, instinctual spirit of the fairies" in *Jonathan Strange and Mr. Norrell* "fundamentally English"—indeed, the novel "is about what it means to be English," although "Clarke's magic is universal."

Jonathan Strange and Mr. Norrell made it to the number three slot on the *New York Times* bestseller list and won numerous awards, including *Time's* Best Novel of the Year in 2004 and the Hugo Award for Best Book in 2005. A made-for-TV series is scheduled for broadcast by the BBC starting in 2014.

Fairies and other magical beings have been an integral part of British mythology and folklore, as well as the mindset of the people, probably since humans set foot on the island. As the amazing success of the twenty-first century books by J.K. Rowling, Neil Gaiman, and Susanna Clarke shows, magic is still alive and well in the UK.

"Faeries, come take me out of
this dull world,

For I would ride with you upon
the wind,

Run on the top of the
dishevelled tide,

And dance upon the mountains
like a flame."

—William Butler Yeats,
The Land of Heart's Desire

CHAPTER 7

Ireland's Feyfolk

o you believe in magic? If you're Irish, or of Irish descent, you probably do. Leprechauns, elves, and other fairies occupy a colorful place in Irish folklore and are considered to play a role in the "luck of the Irish." In fact, many Irish people believe they descended from mystical beings and still have a bit of fairy blood in their veins. Certain families, according to tradition, carry on the royal bloodline of the ancient divinities, and it's their responsibility to safeguard this legacy for the good of humanity and the planet.

The Tuatha dé Danann

Gods and goddesses? Heroes and heroines? Fairies or superhuman beings? Tales of the Tuatha dé Danann are complex and often conflicting. Mythology says these "people of the goddess Danu" are the ancestors of the Irish race and ruled the Emerald Isle in ancient times, led by Danu's son Dagda. They migrated to Ireland from four mystical cities—Falias, Gorias, Finias, and Murias—bringing their knowledge of magic, art, metal-smithing, poetry, music, and healing with them.

Traveling on a cloud, they arrived in Ireland on the eve of Beltane, the pagan fertility holiday, bearing four magic objects or "treasures" given to them by the druids of the four cities:

- ❧ The spear of Lugh, which always struck its mark, emblem of the fire element
- ❧ The stone of destiny, called Lia Fail, which connected the Dananns to the land and enabled them to choose Ireland's kings and queens, signifying the element of earth
- ❧ The sword of Nuada, which brought victory in battle, representing the element of air
- ❧ The cauldron of Dagda, which was never empty and also held healing power, symbolizing the element of water

Magicians today still use these four objects in their work, although usually in a somewhat different manner. You can also find these symbols depicted in the four suits of the tarot.

Legends describe the Dananns as exceptionally beautiful, humanlike in size and form, intelligent and wise. Although supernatural, they often interacted with mortals, sometimes helping and sometimes harming people. They also married humans on occasion. Like many otherworldly beings, they aged very slowly and lived for extended periods of time; however, they weren't immortal.

THE MILESIAN INVASION

In the thirteenth century B.C.E., the Milesians, ancestors of the Gaels, sailed from Spain to Ireland. When the Milesian ships appeared, the Dananns conjured a heavy fog to conceal the Emerald Isle, hoping to avoid attack. But the Mils still managed to overpower the Dananns and forced them to retreat underground, into the magical Otherworld. According to the twelfth-century *Book of Leinster*, the Dananns retaliated by destroying the Mils' grain and souring their milk. Even today, Irish people leave out milk and bread to appease the spirits.

Some sources insist the Tuatha dé Danann continue to live on as deities in exile. Others say that after their defeat at the hands of the Milesians, they degenerated into fairies. Still other researchers propose that the myths surrounding the Tuatha dé Danann symbolize actual human events and the transition from the Bronze Age (the Dananns) to the Iron Age (the Milesians).

Fairy Sightings

Although the Catholic Church tried to stamp out belief in the Tuatha dé Danann, the Irish people continued to revere them. Even St. Patrick is said to have encountered them, according to the twelfth-century *Colloquy with the Ancients*. In Cruachan, County Roscommon, Patrick supposedly saw a beautiful young fairy woman dressed in a green cloak and wearing a golden crown. A ghostly companion told him, "She is of the Tuatha De Danaans who are unfading . . . and I am of the sons of Mil, who are perishable and fade away."

DWELLERS OF THE SACRED MOUNDS

When the Dananns retreated from the Milesians, they took refuge in the hills, burrows, and sacred mounds of Ireland's countryside. They used magic to hide their homes, called sidhe (pronounced *shee*) from human view. Dagda became the fairy king, and his tribe transformed into an invisible and immortal race of magical beings. Over time, the otherworldly inhabitants of these mounds and burrows became identified with their homes and were known as the sidhe.

The Language of the Tuatha dé Danann

The Tuatha dé Danann may have brought ogham to Ireland. In this ancient runic system, the letters of the alphabet correspond to trees—the letters even look like stylized tree trunks with branches sprouting from them. The runes also serve as an oracle to predict the future, with each rune representing a particular concept. Ogham may be written or signed. Throughout Ireland you'll find stones carved with ogham script.

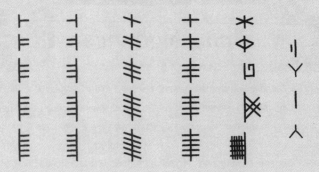

The Sidhe

Having evolved from the Tuatha dé Danann, the sidhe continue to exist as a supernatural race, not exactly divine, but distinct from mortals. Some sources consider them fallen angels. Mythology tells us they diminished in size after people stopped honoring and believing in them, though they retained their humanlike form. Also known as the aos sí, daoine sidhe, and other names in Irish literature, they still maintain contact with the Irish people, especially in rural areas, and protect the land and the lakes.

Like many fairies, they can make themselves invisible or change shape in the blink of an eye. Handsome and aristocratic in bearing, the sidhe organized themselves into tribes or clans, ruled by fairy kings and queens. The Irish people often call them "the Gentry" out of respect. Deep in the burrows beneath their sacred mounds, the sidhe live in magnificent castles made of gold and jewels—hidden from human eyes, of course. There they hold lavish feasts and celebrations, complete with music and dancing. One tale says they store precious gems in a magical place called Sifra, with floors of gold and walls of silver, studded with diamonds.

Want to find the fairies' treasure? On the full moon, walk around a fairy fort nine times and you'll spot the entrance to Sifra. But enter at your own risk, for you may fall under the fairies' spell and never come back from that enchanted place.

The sidhe like to gather at Lough Gur, southeast of the city of Limerick, a beautiful and ancient site with a lovely lake, stone circles, megalithic tombs, and crannogs. According to legend, once every seven years the lake drains, revealing the entrance to Tir na nÓg, the Land of Perpetual Youth. But curious mortals would do well to exercise caution, for at this time the fairy Beann Fhionn drowns one human in the lake and takes him to fairyland.

No doubt you've heard of the Irish bean sidhe (or banshee). The term literally means "woman of the hills," but this female fairy has a frightening reputation. A harbinger of death, she shows up at the home of a person who is about to die, wailing a warning. Often she appears as a crone with long hair and glowing red eyes, wearing a gray mantle over a green dress. Some of the old Irish families even have their very own personal bean sidhe, who lets them know when a relative is about to pass over. In the highly acclaimed Disney movie *Darby O'Gill and the Little People* (1959) starring Sean Connery, a bean sidhe makes a terrifying and unforgettable appearance.

Fairy Sightings

Moyra Doorly, architect and author of *No Place for God*, once spotted a group of nature spirits as they paraded along the banks of a stream. The fairies, whom she dubbed the stripies because they wore green-and-brown striped clothing, were "tall and slender and seemed to move without moving." Imps in bright green garb danced along with the stripies. Doorly followed the fairies, who tried to get her to dress like them, but she refused. They led her into a hall that "looked as if it had been hewn out of rock. There was a long table where preparations for a meal had been made. Again the imps tried to make me change my clothes but I refused. The stripies stood very still, as if in anticipation. Perhaps they were waiting to see if I would sit at their table, which I couldn't bring myself to do. Then I heard the words: 'You are the first person to come this way for 200 years. Come and be with us.' At that I turned away and found myself back at the stream. My impression was that there was nothing in the stripies to 'connect with', that there was something 'absent' about them and an emptiness in their languorous, dreamy air. My impulse was not to linger in their presence or at their table. I might forget too much, too quickly."

"For all the hillside was haunted
By the faery folk come again
And down in the heart-light enchanted
Were opal-coloured men."

—George William Russell, "The Dream of the Children," *AE in the Irish Theosophist*

Fairy Hierarchies

Like humans and deities, fairies divide themselves into hierarchies and social classes. In *Fairy and Folk Tales of the Irish Peasantry*, the noted Irish poet William Butler Yeats referred to two main groups of sidhe: trooping fairies and solitary fairies. (We also find this distinction in the legends of Scotland and Wales.) You could equate them roughly with the ruling and working classes in human society.

TROOPING FAIRIES

Trooping fairies got their name because they travel in long, elaborate processions throughout the countryside. The aristocracy of the Irish fey, they deck themselves out in elegant garments for their parades and play trumpets, harps, and flutes. Some of them mount fairy horses; others ride in splendid chariots. People who have seen the trooping fairies describe their attire as Medieval or Renaissance in style, made from rich fabrics and adorned with gorgeous gems.

These merry folk live and travel in groups. They love getting together for feasts in their grand castles and singing and dancing near ancient stone circles or in groves of trees. Trees, especially hawthorns and oaks, are sacred to them—damage their trees and you'll incur their wrath. Not usually hostile to people, trooping fairies show some interest in human affairs—especially when it comes to stealing objects that appeal to them or playing pranks on mortals.

SOLITARY FAIRIES

As their name implies, solitary fairies prefer to live alone and eschew gatherings of any kind. While the trooping fairies govern the society of the fey, the solitary fairies guard Ireland's fields and forests, lakes and streams. These reclusive, nature-loving beings make their homes in the forests or underwater. The peasants of fairyland, they live simple existences and rarely try to interact with humans—although people occasionally spot them in rural areas. If you come across them it's best to leave them alone—these unfriendly fey can behave in mischievous or malicious ways.

Don't Mess with the Fairies

• •

Before he offended the fairies in 1992, Sean Quinn was the richest man in Ireland, with a fortune of nearly 5 billion euros. But Quinn committed a cardinal crime when he dismantled a 4,000-year-old megalithic burial site known as Aughrim Wedge Tomb near Ballyconnell, County Cavan. Quinn wanted to expand a quarry for his concrete business, and the ancient tomb happened to stand in the way. So he had it removed, stone by stone, to his Slieve Russell Hotel. Since then, Quinn has lost his empire and filed for bankruptcy.

Leprechauns

Leprechauns are synonymous with Ireland—can you imagine Erin without them? Apparently many Irish can't. In 2011, the Cooley Distillery conducted a survey to see if the Irish people believed in leprechauns. More than half said that these crafty creatures lived in the Emerald Isle in the past and a third thought leprechauns still exist today.

Known for their jocular personalities, these clever little men make shoes, stitch clothes, and perform other tasks for the fairy gentry. In fact, they're one of the few fairy types who seem to have regular jobs. Part of the elf clan, they're easy to recognize by their red hair and beards, funny green hats, green suits, and buckled shoes. Sometimes they smoke briar pipes, carry gnarled walking sticks, and tuck shamrocks in their lapels or hat-

bands. Noted musicians, leprechauns enjoy playing fiddles, tin whistles, harps, pipes, and other instruments. They also love to dance jigs.

Most fairies play tricks on humans, but the leprechaun's reputation as a wily prankster surpasses the others'. Not really malicious, these mischievous elves usually do nothing more than cause mishaps around the house, so long as you behave kindly toward them. You can never trust a leprechaun, though—especially when it comes to his legendary pot of gold. Folklore says if you catch this elusive little fellow, he has to tell you where he's hidden his treasure. The odds of actually nabbing him are slim, but if you sneak up behind him while he's at his cobbler's bench busily mending shoes, you might have a chance.

A young Irish farmer named Tom managed to capture a leprechaun and demanded that the fairy reveal the location of his treasure. After some debate, the leprechaun agreed and took Tom to a large field of thistles. He pointed to one plant and told the farmer a big pot of gold was buried beneath that particular thistle. Tom, realizing he'd have to go home for a shovel, tied his red scarf around the thistle plant and made the fairy promise not to touch the thistle or the scarf while he was gone. The leprechaun agreed. Finally, Tom released the fairy, who vanished immediately. Tom hurried home and when he returned to the field, he saw that the leprechaun had kept his word. He hadn't bothered the thistle or the scarf—but he'd tied a red scarf around every thistle plant in the field, and Tom had no idea which one the treasure was buried beneath.

Sporting Leprechauns

The Boston Celtics basketball team chose the leprechaun as their mascot, hoping he'd bring them good luck. Their logo shows him wearing a shamrock-patterned vest and bow tie, smoking a pipe while leaning on a shillelagh, spinning a basketball on his finger, and winking to let you know he's got everything in hand. The leprechaun is also the representative of Notre Dame University's Fighting Irish football team. He's depicted in logo form with his fists up, ready to duke it out with the opponent.

Holly Short

"Stay back, human. You don't know what you're dealing with," warns Holly Short, the daring and delightful police captain of the Lower Elements Police recon (LEPrecon) (pun intended) Unit. She's also an elf.

Just over three feet tall, with short auburn hair, hazel and blue eyes (one of each), and pointed ears, her cuteness makes her seem much younger than her eighty-plus years. She wears a tight green body suit that shows off her slim figure, and oh yes, she can fly. As the protagonist in fantasy novelist Eoin Colfer's bestselling *Artemis Fowl* series, Holly falls victim to, fights, aids, collaborates with, and fancies a twelve-year-old criminal genius named Artemis Fowl, with whom she has a love-hate relationship throughout eight action-packed books. Early in the series, Artemis tries to exploit the fairy world for profit and kidnaps Holly, inciting the wrath of the fairies (never a good thing to do). In later books, Holly and Artemis learn to work together to foil human foes and otherworldly bad guys.

Irish author Colfer also treats young adult readers to a universe of mythical characters, including fairies, trolls, dwarfs, and goblins. The novels, published between 2001 and 2012, have sold more than 21 million copies worldwide, and a feature film based on the first two is in the works.

Although Christianity and industrialism may have caused fairies to lose some ground in Ireland, the people of the Emerald Isle have never given up their faith in the fey. And it's unlikely that they ever will.

"The gods of ancient mythology were changed into the demi-gods and heroes of ancient poetry, and these demi-gods again became, at a later age, the principal characters of our nursery tales."

—Max Müller, German
scholar and philosopher

CHAPTER 8

Northern European Fairies

any of our best-loved fairy tales come from Northern Europe—timeless stories of good and evil, love and longing, strife and salvation, magic and mystery. What Western child doesn't know about *Cinderella*, *Sleeping Beauty*, and *The Little Mermaid*? Although we usually think of the Brothers Grimm and Hans Christian Andersen when we think of Northern European fairy tales, stories of supernatural beings and enchanted lands were handed down by oral tradition—carried from country to country during centuries of migration and conquest—long before these famous writers collected and interpreted them. As you read stories from France, Germany, Scandinavia, and the Netherlands, you'll spot many similarities, which shows that fairies transcend time and national boundaries, delighting children of all ages and cultures.

Madame d'Aulnoy

The term "fairy tale" originated with the French countess Marie-Catherine Le Jumel de Barneville, Baroness d'Aulnoy. A noblewoman by birth, she was married to the Parisian Baron d'Aulnoy at the age of sixteen and began her literary career twenty years later. Her best-known books focused on fairies. Her first story collection, *Les Contes des Fées* (*Tales of Fairies*), was published in 1697, followed a year later by *Contes Nouveaux, ou Les Fées à la Mode* (*New Tales, or Fairies in Fashion*).

Fairy Tales and Feminism

In the mid-seventeenth century, storytelling parlor games became fashionable in Parisian salons. Aristocratic participants took traditional folktales, formerly told by peasants to children in nurseries and considered déclassé, and revised them using wit and imagination to delight one another—and to express ideas that couldn't be discussed in more formal settings. The reworked stories often carried a tantalizing hint of subversiveness when told by nonconformist women dissatisfied with their restricted position in French society. Through this literary medium, they could subtly express ideas about arranged marriages, education for women, financial independence, and other controversial topics of the time. Free thinkers also saw fairy tales as a less constrained and inspired form of literature, distinct from that of the French Academy, an all-boys club devoted to writing in the classical style of ancient Greece and Rome.

Madame d'Aulnoy didn't consider children her audience, although many of her stories featured intriguing animals: a talking white cat, a fairy lioness, an enchanted frog, a magical dolphin. Instead, she wrote her tales for French society's elite, whom she entertained in her rue

Saint-Benoit salon. During the seventeenth century, fairy tales were all the rage among the salon set. Advanced printing techniques made it easier to disseminate stories among the upper classes and to read folklore from other countries. Women authors penned the bulk of literary fairy tales, embellishing older folktales to please the intellectual crowd. As a result, fairy tales increased in popularity and took on a sophisticated tone that appealed to a more educated and moneyed audience.

Charles Perrault and Mother Goose

A contemporary of Madame d'Aulnoy, Charles Perrault gave us Mother Goose and many of the fairy tales we still enjoy today. A leading intellectual of the seventeenth century, Perrault published a volume of eight stories in 1697 titled *Stories or Tales from Times Past, with Morals* or *Tales of Mother Goose*. This collection included "The Sleeping Beauty in the Wood," "Cinderella; or, the Little Glass Slipper," "The Master Cat; or, Puss in Boots," and "Little Red Riding Hood." Perrault wasn't the originator of these fairy tales; they already existed in popular folklore. However, he polished them so they sparkled with style and richness and elevated them to literary status.

MALEFICENT: EVILDOER OR MISUNDERSTOOD FAIRY?

We meet one of Perrault's most famous fairies, the wicked Maleficent, in "Sleeping Beauty." She's the fairy godmother who didn't get an invite to Princess Aurora's christening and who in retribution casts a spell on the baby girl. If Maleficent had gotten her way, the princess would have pricked her finger on a spinning wheel at the age of sixteen and died. But another fairy godmother commutes the sentence; instead of dying, the princess falls into a deep sleep until a prince awakens her with a kiss.

Perrault didn't name the vengeful Maleficent, nor did the Brothers Grimm in their later version of the tale "Little Briar Rose"—in their stories she's simply a wicked fairy. In Tchaikovsky's 1890 ballet, she's called Carabosse. She doesn't actually acquire her name, which means "evildoer," until she steals the show in Disney's 1959 animated feature film. In the 2014 film version, the much-maligned Maleficent (played by Angelina Jolie) finally gets to tell her side of the story.

ENCHANTING WOMEN

In old French romance stories, explains Laura Fry Kready in *A Study of Fairy Tales*, "woman skilled in magic" (i.e., witches) were referred to as fairies. "All those women were called Fays who had to do with enchantment and charms and knew the power and virtue of words, of stones, and of herbs, by which they were kept in youth and in great beauty and in great riches."

Absinthe: The Green Fairy

Is this seductive beauty truly a fairy? Or a hallucination brought on by the potent drink that bears her name? Myth says the wicked Greek fairy Circe taught The Green Fairy how to concoct her secret potion, and that her special elixir is even more intoxicating than the alcoholic beverage. The quintessential artists' muse, absinthe—the liquor and/or the fairy—inspired many of the world's great creative geniuses, including Oscar Wilde, Toulouse-Lautrec, Picasso, Manet, Van Gogh, Gauguin, and Baudelaire. A combination of wormwood, anise, and fennel, traditional absinthe has a much higher alcohol content (55 to 75 percent) than whisky (40 percent) and derives its characteristic green color from various herbs added after distillation. During the early 1900s, France, Switzerland, the United States, and other countries outlawed absinthe, but the United States lifted its ban in 2007.

Beauty and the Beast

Half a century after Madame d'Aulnoy made her writing debut, another Frenchwoman of the elite salon set, Gabrielle-Suzanne Barbot de Villeneuve, penned the bittersweet fairy tale "La Belle et la Bête." Sixteen years later, author Jeanne-Marie Le Prince de Beaumont published her shorter and better-known version, and in 1771 the operatic interpretation of the tale, *Zémire et Azor*, became a resounding hit.

In this enduring story, a bankrupt merchant picks a rose from the garden of a fearsome beast to take home to his youngest daughter, Belle. The hideous beast, in return for sparing the man's life, demands that he send Belle to live in the beast's castle. When she arrives, the beast lavishes the beautiful young maiden with the finest food, clothing, and accommodations and asks her to marry him, but

she refuses. Despite the luxuries she enjoys in her life with the beast, Belle grows homesick and he lets her go visit her family. But when she doesn't return as promised, the heartbroken beast nearly dies from grief. Stricken with guilt, Belle hurries back to the castle and tells the dying beast that she loves him—and when her tears fall on his grotesque body, he magically transforms into a handsome prince.

In Villeneuve's version, both Belle and the beast have fairy connections. Belle's real father is a king and her mother is a fairy. The beast is an enchanted prince reared by a wicked and seductive fairy who wants him to be her lover. When he refuses, she turns him into a monster. Beaumont's version contains a particularly nasty bit in which Belle's two evil sisters plot to keep Belle from returning to the beast until he gets angry enough to eat her—a little aside that doesn't make it into contemporary tellings.

The story, of course, shows that when you truly love someone, you don't care about outer appearances. It also carries the message "don't judge a book by its cover." Jungian analysts have interpreted the beast as representing a person's "shadow" side, which must be accepted and loved in order for psychological health and happiness to exist.

Comtesse de Ségur's Fairy Tales

In 2009, Project Gutenberg made *Old French Fairy Tales*, penned by the Comtesse de Ségur in the mid-nineteenth century, available as an eBook. Although born in Russia, the Comtesse moved to France with her family when she was eighteen. There she married the French count Eugène Henri Raymond. Best known as a novelist, she also excelled at writing fairy tales, and her delightful collection is magnificently illustrated in color and black and white by artist Virginia Frances Sterrett. You can read or download this lovely book free by visiting *www.gutenberg.org*.

The Brothers Grimm

The work of the German brothers Jacob and Wilhelm Grimm dominates the Western world's body of fairy tale literature. From their initial publications in the early 1800s until well into the twentieth century, their books ranked second only to the Bible in terms of popularity in Germany. The Grimms' first collection, *Children's and Household Tales* (1812), contained 86 tales and was later expanded to include 200. Despite the title, however, these stories weren't just for children and often contained gruesome details that might give kids horrifying nightmares. Many of the stories published in the Grimms' collections originated in oral tradition; earlier writers, including French literary luminaries Madame d'Aulnoy and Charles Perrault, had revised, translated, and compiled these timeless tales into anthologies more than a century before the Grimms got into the act.

The nature of fairy tales is to evolve over time and to portray eternal themes that resonate with people of all cultures and time periods. The Brothers Grimm became famous for adapting folktales such as "Snow White," "Hansel and Gretel," "The Frog Prince," "Cinderella," and "Rumplestiltskin" for a receptive German audience. In addition to presenting moral guidance to children, the fairy tales touched on sociopolitical issues of the times, cloaked in the guise of fantasy. The Grimms' stories resonated with German nationalism, which led the Nazis to use them in their propaganda campaigns during World War II.

What did the Grimm brothers intend to accomplish by compiling ancient folklore into storybook collections for the intelligentsia? According to Harvard professor Maria Tatar, they hoped to preserve what they considered an important piece of German history and literature during a time of chaos and uncertainty. But because the Grimms came from the academic class, they had little understanding of the peasants who had originated and preserved fairy tales over the centuries, and like the French collectors before them, they put a literary gloss on old folklore. Like all researchers, the Brothers Grimm also infused traditional folktales with their own personal biases, which included racism, sexism, and able-ism.

Fairy Tale Tours

Want to visit the land of the German fairies? The German Fairy Tale Route takes you through 600 kilometers (373 miles) of Medieval villages, enchanted castles, and spectacular countryside that inspired the Brothers Grimm. Explore river valleys, forests, and mountain ranges on foot or bicycle to get the most from this magical tour. See *www.deutsche-maerchenstrasse.com* for more information.

Another Perspective on German Fairy Tales

Historian Franz Xaver von Schönwerth, a contemporary of the Brothers Grimm, also collected German folklore, myths, and legends. For decades, von Schönwerth traveled around in the Bavarian region of Oberpfalz, talking with people of the lower classes in rural areas—servants, laborers, farmers, etc.—and compiled their oral tales into three volumes titled *Sitten und Sagen aus der Oberpfalz* (1857, 1858, 1859). Unlike the Grimms, von Schönwerth recounted the stories told to him in the peasants' vernacular—which may be why his books never gained popularity and were soon forgotten.

Then, in 2011, cultural curator Erika Eichenseer discovered 500 fairy tales gathered by von Schönwerth that had been stashed away for 150 years in an archive in Regensburg, Germany. Many of these stories had never been published elsewhere. According to Eichenseer, von Schönwerth made no attempt to polish, interpret, or romanticize the tales; he presented them as the locals told them to him. "Their main purpose was to help young adults on their path to adulthood," she says, "showing them that dangers and challenges can be overcome through virtue, prudence and courage."

Professor Daniel Drascek of the University of Regensburg calls von Schönwerth's work "the most significant collection in the German-speaking world in the 19th century," surpassing even the Grimms'. At present, von Schönwerth's books are being translated into English.

German Fairies

Germany has its share of trolls, elves, and gnomes, but in some cases, these beings behave differently than they do in other countries. Mischievous German elves, for instance, bring nightmares—the German word *Altraum* means "elf-dream."

Additionally, some distinctive fairy folk not found elsewhere call Germany home.

KOBOLDS

Small in stature and ugly in appearance, these fairies dwell in mines. Some sources, including historian Thomas Keightley, link the kobold to the British brownies, who come out of hiding at night to help humans with household chores. Known as pranksters who aggravate mortals, kobolds aren't evil, just mischievous.

THE TRICKY NIXIE

This shapeshifting spirit lives in lakes, rivers, and waterfalls but can assume human form to come on land. Known for their great beauty, nixies also have exquisite voices and play a mean violin, with which they entice mortals. Sometimes the fairies marry humans, but they also drown people.

RÜBEZABL

A solitary fairy named Rübezabl is said to roam the German countryside. He can command sunshine or snow and conjures freak storms when it suits his purposes. By some accounts, he appears as a rugged-looking backwoods elf, though he's capable of changing his shape. Ordinarily unfriendly to humans, he sometimes rewards those who show him respect by giving them precious gems or gold.

MOSS MAIDENS

These tiny, benevolent nature spirits understand the healing properties of plants. Diligent spinners, their job is to weave the moss found at the base of trees and on the forest floor.

DER GROSSMAN

One of those morality spirits who scares kids into obedience, this Black Forest fairy grabs unruly children at night and drags them into the woods. There he harasses them until they admit their misbehavior.

LORELEI

On a rock above the Rhine River near Sankt Goarshausen sits a dangerous water spirit named Lorelei. Like mermaids and other river nymphs, her enchanting voice lures boatmen to their deaths.

The Erlking

The dark forests of Germany gave rise to a number of equally dark legends. Chief among these are the horrifying tales of the Erlking, or fairy king. This creature lurks in the depths of forests, pursuing lone travelers and carrying them off to their deaths.

Among the most frightening depictions of the creature was that of Johann Goethe in his poem "The Erl King," later set to music by the composer Franz Schubert. In the gathering darkness, a man rides in fear through the forest, sheltering his young child:

> *"My son, wherefore seek'st thou thy face thus to hide?"*
> *"Look, father, the Erl King is close by our side!*
> *Dost see not the Erl King with crown and train?"*
> *"My son, 'tis the mist rising over the plain."*

Despite the father's calming words, the child can hear the soft and cunning voice of the fairy spirit whispering in his ears.

> *"Oh, come, thou dear infant! oh come thou with me!*
> *Full many a game I will play there with thee;*
> *On my strand, lovely flowers their blossoms unfold,*
> *My mother shall grace thee with garments of gold."*

The child resists, and once again the father calms him with soothing words, but the erlking will not be denied his prey.

> *"I love thee, I'm charm'd by thy beauty, dear boy!*
> *And if thou'rt unwilling, then force I'll employ."*
> *"My father, my father, he seizes me fast,*
> *Full sorely the Erl-King has hurt me at last."*
> *The father now gallops, with terror half wild,*
> *He grasps in his arms the poor shuddering child;*
> *He reaches his courtyard with toil and with dread,*
> *The child in his arms finds he motionless, dead."*

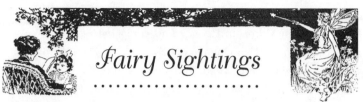

Fairy Sightings

At Schweizersbild near Schaffhausen, Switzerland, researchers in 1893 discovered the skeletons of dwarfs, which seemed clear evidence that these mythological beings existed and that fairies weren't merely figments of folklore and fantasy. More dwarf skeletons turned up at Spy, Belgium. Professor Fraipont described the Spy skeletons as very short, with "voluminous heads, massive bodies, short arms and bent legs." Further examination showed that these beings lived in caves and formed tools from flint.

Will-o'-the-Wisps

If you stray near a bog on a dark night, you may glimpse small lights flickering over its surface, half hidden among the reeds. Travelers, beware! You've encountered will-o'-the-wisps, among the most dangerous of fairies who lure unwary wayfarers to their deaths.

Authorities are divided as to whether these fairy spirits represent malevolent otherworldly beings or the souls of unfortunates who died unbaptized. In Wales, they are said to be púcas, who lead travelers into the marsh and leave them there to die. However, in some Northern European cultures, the will-o'-the-wisps' lights mark the site of buried treasure. (This belief also exists in central Europe, and Bram Stoker's great classic horror novel *Dracula* mentions it in the opening chapters.)

Will-o'-the-wisps can create frightening, eerie sounds to scare their victims. Versions of the phenomenon exist in virtually all cultures, ranging from the Boitatá of Brazil to the Aleya, or ghost-light, of Bengal. John Milton, in *Paradise Lost*, compared Satan to a will-o'-the-wisp when the Evil One tempts Eve to stray from the path and taste the forbidden fruit. Tolkien employed will-o'-the-wisps as denizens of the Dead Marshes, who mislead the hobbits Frodo and Sam as they make their way toward the Black Land of Mordor. And, not surprisingly, they pop up in the Harry Potter stories.

Hans Christian Andersen

Best known for his story about another mythical creature—The Little Mermaid—Hans Christian Andersen occupies a prominent place in the world of fairy tale literature. "Life itself is the most wonderful fairy tale," the Danish writer stated, and in his case it was true. As the character in his famous story "The Ugly Duckling" was born ugly but became beautiful when he was an adult swan, Andersen was born into poverty but rose to a position of fame and fortune. He hobnobbed with royalty, traveled as a celebrity far and wide, and left a legacy known throughout the world.

As a boy, Andersen learned folklore from old women who worked with his grandmother at an insane asylum in his hometown of Odense. After a difficult youth during which he struggled unsuccessfully to become an actor or singer, he published his first collection of fairy tales in 1835, at the age of twenty-nine. Influenced by *The Thousand and One Nights*, as well as the French fairy tales told in Parisian salons and the work of the Brothers Grimm, Andersen also drew on old Danish folktales for inspiration but wove original narratives around the basic plots. Often dark, laced with satire and comedy,

Andersen's fairy tales incorporated his personal experiences. His stories revolutionized children's literature in Denmark, taking them out of the realm of pedantic moralizing and into the bright world of magic. Today, the most prestigious award for children's literature bears his name: The Hans Christian Andersen Medal.

Norse Mythology: The Root of Scandinavian Fairy Tales

Hammer-wielding Thor, Odin the wisdom-bearer, the sensual fertility goddess Freya, the trickster Loki—the adventures of these and other ancient Norse deities provided the fertile soil from which Scandinavian fairy tales sprouted.

Norse myths often depict gods and goddesses interacting with fairies. Thor, for instance, goes on expeditions to battle trolls. Freya loves beautiful things and does what's necessary to obtain them— she sleeps with four dwarfs, which nets her a bird-feather cloak that enables her to shapeshift into a falcon, a rare and valuable necklace, and a chariot drawn by two magical cats. She's also a big fan of fairies and commands the valkyries. Loki, in "The Volsunga Saga," steals a ring that belongs to a dwarf—an act that has a parallel in J.R.R. Tolkien's *Lord of the Rings*.

In one such tale, the god Odin fears that Fenrir, the fierce and unruly wolf-child of Loki, poses a threat to the Æsir (Norse deities). After several failed attempts to chain the wolf, Odin meets with the fairy king of Alfheim, who admits he has no experience fighting monsters, having spent his life in the forest among the plants, birds, and animals. However, as a result of observing the power in small things, he thinks he might be able to help rein in the dangerous beast Fenrir. The fairy offers to enlist the help of dwarfs, and Odin agrees.

After two days' work, the dwarfs produce a surprisingly delicate chain made of six amazing ingredients, including the footfalls of cats and the voices of fish, with which to bind the wolf. The mighty Fenrir, scoffing at the seemingly fragile chain, allows the Æsir to slip it over his neck—a mistake, as it turns out, for the more he struggles the tighter the chain grows. Thus the fairy's magic intervenes in the affairs of the gods and keeps them from harming each other.

Scandinavian Fairies

The legends of Norway, Sweden, and Denmark describe a plethora of fairies and otherworldly beings—some also turn up in the folklore of other regions and some are unique to Scandinavia. Trolls, especially, get a lot more attention in these Northern European countries than in other parts of the world, whereas tiny winged beings barely warrant a mention.

TROLLS

Large, ugly, dull-witted, lumbering, and hairy, trolls don't get the good parts in fairy tales, which might contribute to their dislike of humans. Even in contemporary role-playing fantasy games, they appear as horrible and heartless monsters. However, trolls can change shape and appear quite handsome when they want to charm humans—especially women, whom they capture as wives. If you leave them alone they're usually not dangerous, but they can become ferocious if you taunt them. Rich trolls make their homes in the mountains, where they stash great stores of gold and silver; the poor ones live in the forests or under bridges, as you'll recall from the Norwegian tale "The Three Billy Goats Gruff." Extremely sensitive to sunlight, trolls turn to stone when exposed to the light of day.

The Trouble with Trolls

Trolls don't get a lot of good press, and they're often portrayed as ugly, stupid, or both. The trouble is, descriptions of what they look like and what they do vary dramatically, making it hard for mortals to recognize or understand them. J.R.R. Tolkien, for example, portrays them as huge, humanlike beings who stand about nine feet tall. Terry Pratchett in the Discworld books calls trolls violent creatures made of stone whose intelligence wanes in warm weather. Jan Brett's *Trouble with Trolls* depicts trolls as smallish in stature and able to withstand sunlight. The Harry Potter stories describe them as bloodthirsty, murderous giants. Bill Peet's *Jethro and Joel Were a Troll* features a two-headed troll who seems immune to sunshine and helps people by building castles for them.

Fantasy games, too, differ in their interpretations of trolls. In Dungeons & Dragons, trolls are tall, thin, green-skinned goons who can only be permanently harmed if burned by fire or acid. Earthdawn's trolls, however, get better treatment, appearing as large, powerful, decent guys with horns and copious body hair.

BERGRESAR

Ancestors of trolls, these ancient, huge, and powerful beings represent chaos. They dislike just about everybody, including humans, elves, and deities. Churches and bells annoy them too, and they hurl boulders to destroy church buildings.

ALVER

These Swedish elves come in two varieties: ljósálfar (light elves) and døkkálfar (dark elves). The beautiful, fair-skinned light elves live in the sky—they're the good alver. The coal-black dark elves—the bad guys—live in the earth. The ljósálfar inspired J.R.R. Tolkien's race of wise elves.

"I met a little Elf-man once
Down where the lilies blow.
I asked him why he was so small,
And why he didn't grow.
He slightly frowned, and with his eye
He looked me through and through.
'I'm quite as big for me,' said he,
'As you are big for you.' "

—John Kendrick Bangs, "The Little Elf"

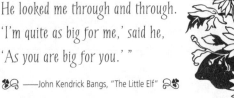

HAVMAN AND HAVFRUE

These beautiful blue-skinned water spirits resemble merfolk and are generally benevolent creatures. They guide seafarers safely through Scandinavia's waterways and sometimes come ashore to find mortal mates.

THE TRÄDANDAR

The spirits of trees, these deities live among the branches and communicate by rustling the leaves. They can shapeshift into owls, women, or tiny fairies who dance in the treetops. Legends say that when people die their souls become tree spirits.

DVÄRGAR

Known as master craftsmen who fashioned Odin's spear, Thor's hammer, and Frey's ship, these small, ugly male spirits live in cliffs and abhor people. When they don magic cloaks or hats they become invisible.

GÅRDSTOMTE

This hard-working spirit helps farmers by caring for livestock and doing chores around the homestead. Usually depicted as an old man with a long, white beard and peasant's clothing, he likes porridge and gets angry if people don't take good care of their property and animals.

THE VALKYRIES

One of the better-known Scandinavian spirits, these female entities decide which warriors survive and which die on the battlefield. They ride into the fray on flying horses, then ferry half the dead to Odin's Valhalla and half to Fólkvangr, home of the goddess Freya. As they cross into the world of the deities, they cause the Northern Lights to illuminate the sky.

Today's fairy tales, whether updated versions of old favorites or new stories geared toward contemporary readers, still teach values to young people and offer them guidance as they grapple with life's challenges. However, Wolfgang Mieder, professor of German and folklore at the University of Vermont and winner of the 2012 European Fairytale Prize, expresses concern that the amazing array of fairy tales on the market today lets people read lots of different stories instead of sharing the same ones, the way our ancestors did. The power of connection that storytelling offered previous generations is waning.

Nonetheless, Mieder feels optimistic about the future of fairy tales. "In fairytales, age-old problems—normal, day-to-day problems people have—are allegorized in a poetic, symbolic language," he says. "We can identify with one another across boundaries."

"Where round the bed, whence Achelous springs,

That wat'ry Fairies dance in mazy rings."

—Homer, *Iliad*

CHAPTER 9

Southern European Fairies

ust as many of our oldest myths come from the Mediterranean countries, so do our oldest fairy tales. Among people who lived near the sea, water fairies or nymphs dominated folklore and legends, as might be expected. The Greek author Homer wrote about these beguiling beauties in his epic poems the *Iliad* and the *Odyssey* back in the late-eighth and early-seventh centuries B.C.E. The people of Southern Europe also had their versions of earth and water elementals—who lived in caves, forests, or waterways—and even some winged beings. And of course, the ominous Fates who meted out human destiny originated with the Greeks and migrated around the coast, showing up as the norns in Roman life and the fada in Spain. As seems to be the case in the fairy tales of most cultures, the cast of characters includes both friendly and ferocious spirits.

The Fates

Greek mythology portrays the Fates, also known as the Moirae, as three sisters who determine our destiny: the length, quality, and other particulars of our lives. They dole out rewards and punishments, happiness and misery, triumph and tragedy. Naturally, these ladies command respect and awe—although it's rumored that Zeus really calls the shots and passes along his decisions to the Fates to enact. The eldest sister, Clotho, spins the thread from which human life is formed. Lachesis, the second sister, measures the thread and determines how long a life will last and what a person's lot in life will entail. Atropos, the youngest, cuts the thread at the moment of death. Another sister, Tyche, appears in some tales as the Fate of Fortune, who hands out beauty, luck, virtue, and fame.

Usually depicted as wizened hags, the Fates keep careful records of human activities and life on earth, engraving everything on indestructible brass and iron tablets. These accounts will endure throughout eternity. No one, not even the gods, escapes the Fates. According to some sources, Zeus, chief of the Olympians—the Leader of the Fates—doesn't bow to destiny, though others say even the great Zeus must obey what the sisters decree. When he fell in love with a nereid (a saltwater spirit) named Thetis, the Fates warned that if the couple had a son, the child would grow up to be more powerful than his father. Zeus, not wanting his son to overthrow him, decided to marry Thetis off to

someone else: a mortal named Peleus. The couple became parents of the great Achilles, hero of the Trojan War (in fact, the events that were to lead to the war began at the marriage of Thetis and Peleus). So it seems that even the top god takes orders from the Fates.

The Furies

The ancient Greeks feared the Furies even more than the Fates. These fairy sisters meted out justice and punishment and drove mortals mad. People who murdered family members reaped the worst of their torment, maybe because the Fates themselves arose from the blood of Uranus when his son Cronus overthrew him. Mythology mentions three Furies in particular: Alecto (endless), Tisiphone (punishment), and Megaera (jealous rage). Supremely ugly, these vengeful fairies had black wings and skin, hair made of snakes, and really bad body odor—sometimes they shapeshifted into swarms of insects.

Only wrongdoers, however, had to worry about the Furies. According to legends, they left innocent people alone. Mainly they wanted to see justice served, and even someone guilty of a violent crime might escape their torture if the Furies considered the act warranted. That's what happens in the play *Eumenides*. Orestes kills his mother because she participated in the murder of his father, King Agamemnon of Mycenae. The Furies demand that he stand trial, but they accept the verdict of justifiable homicide.

Greek Water Fairies

"They spring from fountains and from sacred groves/And holy streams that flow into Rübezabl the sea." So wrote the poet Homer, nearly 3,000 years ago. In those days, nubile nymphs frolicked in every available water source—lakes, rivers, seas, waterfalls, even fountains and wells. The Greeks categorized these nature fairies according to their habitat. Too many varieties exist to mention here, but if you want to see a more complete list visit *www.theoi.com*.

NYMPHS

In ancient Greece, naiads lived in flowing fresh water (streams, springs). Nereids preferred the salty seas (Aegean, Adriatic, Mediterranean). Oceanids, as the name implies, called the ocean home. Depicted as lovely and benevolent creatures, nymphs sometimes mated with gods and even humans—including a number of characters in Homer's *Iliad*.

THE SIRENS

Unlike the sweet-tempered nymphs, these seductive water spirits sang so divinely that they drove men wild with desire. Crazed seafarers jumped into the ocean to meet the magnificent maidens and subsequently drowned. Perhaps the most famous example comes from Homer's *Odyssey*, in which the hero Odysseus orders his men to tie him to the mast of his ship so the sirens won't lure him to a watery grave.

CIRCE

When Helios, the sun king, mated with an oceanid, the result was a fairy of the not-so-nice variety: Circe. She earned herself a bad reputation in Greek folklore for turning Odysseus's crew into pigs. A master magician, she was also known for concocting mysterious potions, some poisonous and some that kept her eternally young. For thousands of years, Circe lived on the island of Aeaea where legends say she still enjoys sinking ships.

Earth Fairies

In old Greek legends, countless earth fairies lived in the forests—and they were quite particular about which trees they chose for their homes. Like the water nymphs, the tree fairies were named according to their habitats. They protected the woodlands, as forest fairies elsewhere do, and unless humans encroached on their homeland they usually left mortals alone. We also find human-animal hybrid creatures in Greek lore, as well as dragons, giants, and assorted monsters, usually the products of mixed-species parents.

THE DRYADS

These forest fairies serve the hunter-goddess Artemis as her companions and attendants. They prefer to live in oaks and willows, and protect the woodlands. Usually playful and harmless to humans, they only show themselves to mortals when they're angry—so if you see one, back off fast. If you need to appease them, try offering them wine, olive oil, or honey.

HAMADRYADS

A special type of dryad, these tree fairies actually embody trees and animate them, especially oaks and poplars in sacred groves. They penalize or reward humans, depending on how the humans treat plants. If a tree dies naturally or is cut down, the hamadryad's soul departs at the same time. In an old Greek fairy tale, a man named Rhœcus comes upon an oak that's about to fall down and props it up, thereby saving the hamadryad who would have died along with the tree. To reward him for his kindness, the fairy becomes his lover.

OREADES, MELIAI, AND OTHER TREE FAIRIES

According to Greek folklore, different types of fairies live in different types of trees. All these wood nymphs are beautiful, gentle creatures. Oreades, for instance, inhabit and protect pines, firs, spruces, and other conifers. Meliai are the spirits of ash trees; maliades guard fruit trees; daphnaie live in laurels, and so on. Every tree has a nymph in residence.

SATYRS AND SILENI

Half-goat, half-man, the satyr makes his home in the woods and mountains, hanging out with the god Dionysus. These guys spend much of their time drinking, dancing, and running around after female fairies (and sometimes humans). Also companions of Dionysus, the sileni are described as fat, ugly, bald drunks and lechers, with only one redeeming quality: their musical talent. Like satyrs, the sileni sometimes appear as composite beings, usually part horse, part man—similar to centaurs, but not as good-looking.

Fairies of the Air

According to the Neo-Platonist Porphyry, who lived in Greece during the third century, spirits of all kinds, benevolent and malevolent, flew through the skies. They had no definite shape, but could assume whatever appearance they chose. He described the evil ones as "composed of turbulent malignity." If mortals didn't show them the proper respect, the disgruntled fairies might wreak havoc in the offenders' lives. Like water and earth spirits, different types of fairies embody different types of air. The lovely aurae, for instance, waft along on the cool morning breezes, whereas the harpyiae swirl in whirlwinds and anemoi stir up storms. Nephelae float in the clouds.

Sylphs, a name that originates in the Greek word *silphe*, are often presented in Greek mythology as symbols of purity, intellect, and freedom, as well as the spirits that transcend human existence and connect us to the divine realms. Air, of course, is essential for life, and these airy fairies enable humans to inhale this vital ingredient. The next time you're in a quiet spot in nature, take a moment to listen to the wind upon which the air spirits ride. You may hear them whispering their secrets among the rustling of leaves, as they've done for countless centuries.

"Of course you don't believe in fairies. You're fifteen. You think I believed in fairies at fifteen? Took me until I was at least a hundred and forty. Hundred and fifty, maybe."

— Neil Gaiman, *The Sandman, Vol. 6: Fables and Reflections*

Fairies of Ancient Rome and Italy

Like the Greeks, the early Romans believed beautiful nymphs occupied the waters of the world. Certain nymphs, including the lymphae and luturna, enjoyed deity-like status because they brought the life-giving rains. The nymphs Egeria and Opis were birth divinities, to whom expectant mothers or women who wished to become pregnant prayed and made offerings. The Romans, who co-opted many of the Greek divinities, also had their version of the Fates, known as the Parcae or the Fata. Individually, the sisters were called Nona, Decima, and Morta.

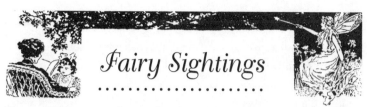

Fairy Sightings

Pliny the Younger, a magistrate of ancient Rome, supposedly wrote a letter to Roman Senator Licinius Sura in which he conveyed an intriguing story that took place circa c.e. 79. According to Pliny, a boy gazing at a fresco of a grand city in his parents' home noticed in the painting a figure of a man that he'd never seen there before. Suddenly, the man moved! The figure wore "a tunic made of the Deeds of Ancestors, fastened with a belt of Piety, sandals made from good Fortune and Wise Decisions and a toga woven of Citizenship." The boy asked the man if he were a lar, and the fairy admitted he was. Then the lar outstretched his hand and led the boy into the painting, where the two of them walked about the streets of the city. The lar, who visited this place often, spoke to many people in the painting and those people greeted the boy, too. After observing many wondrous sights, the lar guided the mortal back to his home and said farewell, promising to return.

Several weeks later, the lar appeared in a different fresco and again invited the boy to join him within the painting. Again, the lar and the boy lived the events shown in the fresco. This happened once more, with the lar and the boy journeying into a pastoral scene depicted in yet another fresco. This time, however, the boy ate an orange from a tree in that world, as well as olives and grapes they gathered along their way. At the end of their adventure, the boy tried to emerge from the fresco and reenter his ordinary world. But as he did, he saw Mount Vesuvius erupting and, in shock, released the lar's hand. The boy was never again seen in this world.

Perhaps the most common fairy in ancient Rome, however, was the lar, a household guardian spirit connected to an individual family. Some folklore says these fairies were the spirits of men who'd died and returned to protect the homes where they'd once lived. Every family had its lar. According to legend, lares enjoy celebrations and festivities of all kinds and expect the families with whom they reside to honor them with small shrines and gifts.

The early Italians also recognized fairy elementals, who served as representatives of their respective realms: earth, air, fire, and water. Nymphs fell into the category of water elementals. Earth elementals known as erdluitle, like the dwarfs and trolls of Northern Europe, lived in caves and underground burrows, where they skillfully fashioned implements out of metal. Other earth elementals called the silvanni resided in the forests and groves, and protected trees. Winged sylphs, the playful air elementals who resemble our modern-day concept of fairies, were known in Italy as the folletti. The fouchi fatui or fire fairies looked like small flames; the benevolent ones guarded hearth fires, but the mischievous fairies led people astray with their sparkling lights.

Where Can You Find Fairies in Contemporary Italy?

In today's industrialized world, where do nature-loving fairies hang out? Legend says they're attracted to a beautiful and peaceful lake in Italy's western Alps near the Monte Rosa, appropriately called Lago delle Fate or "Fairies' Lake." You might also seek them in a hill in Abruzzi (central Italy) named Colle delle Fate (Fairies' Hill) and a nearby cave called Grotta delle Fate (Fairies' Cave). A mountain peak called Monte delle Fate (Fairies' Mountain) in the Monti Ausoni range of southern Lazio is also rumored to house fairies. And in Tuscany, fairies are said to retreat to fairy holes or underground caves called *buche delle fate* during the cold winter months, where they spin and weave garments—or perhaps the future of the human race.

Giovanni Francesco "Gianfrancesco" Straparola

The earliest-known versions of some of our favorite fairy tales came from the pen of the Italian writer Giovanni Francesco Straparola. His surname, probably a pseudonym, means "babbler." In the mid-sixteenth century, Straparola published a collection of fairy tales, *Le piacevoli notti* (*The Facetious Nights*), which contained 75 stories, including the earliest known version of "Puss in Boots."

Like *The Canterbury Tales* and *The Thousand and One Nights*, the collection includes a frame story that provides a reason for various characters to swap stories—in this case a party on the island of Murano just outside Venice, famous for its glassworks since the tenth century. Because many literate artisans lived in Venice at that time, Straparola's collection presented tales of ordinary people succeeding financially and advancing socially; thus Straparola used the vehicle of fairy tales to comment on the tenor of the times.

Giambattista Basile

Charles Perrault and the Brothers Grimm were undoubtedly influenced by the Italian poet Giambattista Basile, who eighty years after publication of Straparola's collections (and 200 years prior to the Grimms') brought together versions of many popular European tales in two volumes titled *Il Pentamerone* (*The Tale of Tales, or Entertainment for Little Ones*). Published in 1634 and 1636, after his death and under the pen name Gian Alesio Abbatutis, *Pentamerone* wasn't translated into English until the mid-1800s.

A frame story holds together forty-nine other tales, told over a period of time. "The Sun, Moon, and Talia" was the predecessor to "Sleeping Beauty," with a few unsavory differences. Instead of a disgruntled fairy godmother cursing the young girl, Talia's father consults her horoscope and foresees the deathlike sleep she falls into when she gets a flax splinter in her finger. Years later, a king enters the home where Talia lies comatose and rapes her, impregnating her with twins. After she gives birth, one of the babies sucks the splinter out of her finger, allowing her to waken. When the king's wife finds out about it, she orders the twins brought to her, planning to cook them and feed them to her philandering husband. However, the cook hides the children and serves the king two lambs instead. Then the jealous queen invites Talia to visit, intending to burn the girl alive when she arrives. The king, though, discovers his wife's plot and has her burned instead. At the end of the story, Talia and the king marry—but this happily-ever-after tale contains too much nastiness to be romantic.

Basile's collection also features stories similar to "Cinderella," "Puss in Boots," "Hansel and Gretel," "Snow White," and "Rapunzel." Later adaptations of these dark, violent, and sometimes coarse tales have been sanitized and sweetened to provide more acceptable entertainment for youngsters.

The Blue Fairy in *Pinocchio*

Fairies and fairy tales flourished in Italy during the late nineteenth century, just as they did in other European countries. One of the favorite stories, then and now, features a marionette who wants to become a human boy and whose nose grows whenever he tells a lie. The novel *The Adventures of Pinocchio* by Carlo Collodi (real name Carlo Lorenzini) was published in weekly installments in the first Italian newspaper devoted to children. In it, the adventurous protagonist repeatedly gets himself into troublesome situations, but fortunately for him, he has a fairy guardian by his side: the Fairy with Turquoise Hair (later renamed the Blue Fairy in Disney's animated film version).

Like many old fairy tales, this one comes with a moral for young readers: behave yourself, don't engage in bad or dangerous behavior, and tell the truth. Although the Blue Fairy keeps issuing this warning to Pinocchio, the mischievous puppet doesn't listen to her, at least in the beginning of the story. Pinocchio meets the fairy in the forest, where she's lived for 1,000 years. This benevolent being continues to rescue Pinocchio from the wild and amusing plights he gets himself into. First, a fox and a cat hang him from a tree and she frees him. Later, he's magically transformed into a donkey and thrown into the ocean, but the good fairy intervenes and changes him back into a puppet. Her turquoise hair (blue fur in one embodiment as a mountain goat) enables Pinocchio to recognize her. Despite the puppet's willful disregard for her advice, she continues to take care of him. At the end of the tale, the fairy benefactor gives a house to a talking cricket, and Pinocchio and his aged father, the wood-carver Geppetto, move in with the cricket. In her final gesture of generosity, the fairy transforms Pinocchio from a puppet into a real boy and, in the bargain, makes him rich by changing his copper coins into gold.

Disney, in the 1940 animated film adaptation of the book, removed the fairy's most striking feature: her turquoise hair. Instead, she's portrayed as a beautiful blonde wearing a blue gown. Another treatment of the story in 1987, *Pinocchio and the Emperor of the Night*, restores the fairy's blue hair and adds several new twists and turns to the plot, including a girl named Twinkle, who's been transformed into a puppet. In Steven Spielberg's 2001 sci-fi movie *A.I. Artificial Intelligence*, the Blue Fairy makes another appearance, this time as a statue at Coney Island, which the android protagonist mistakes for the real fairy. In all these versions, the lovely fairy comes off as a compassionate and likable character—nothing like the trickster fey in many other fairy tales and legends. A new, darker interpretation of *Pinocchio* by director Guillermo del Toro is scheduled for release in 2014.

The Spanish Duende

Psychoanalysts could have a field day with the Spanish duende. Is it a fairy? A part of the human psyche? Or a force that exists in the universe that sparks the creative spirit?

Derived, perhaps, from the folklore of the Moors and the Middle East and brought to Spain by gypsies, the Spanish duende is a colorful conundrum. Some people insist it's impossible to explain.

One perspective describes this mysterious spirit as similar to a hobgoblin, a trickster like the Irish leprechaun who hands out fairy gold that soon disappears. The duende looks like a small old man dressed in gray or dark clothing, with only one eye and one nostril. An annoying little guy, he makes noises and hurls stones at people. Other accounts connect the duende with fallen angels and demons. Like all fairies, he casts spells on mortals and can lock them in a trancelike state for a period of time.

Some stories recount incidents of the duende stealing children—as fairies in other lands are known to do—though often this happens when the parents don't seem to value or enjoy their offspring. In the fairy tale "The Daughter of Peter de Cabinam," an impatient father wishes demons would carry off his crying child. He gets his wish, and the daughter is spirited away to the top of a mountain in Catalonia where demons live in a palace at the bottom of an infinitely deep lake. In another tale, "Origin of the House of Haro," a fairy married to a mortal husband snatches away their daughter when the man breaks his promise to her.

The Flamenco Spirit

The poet Federico Garcia Lorca considered the duende a feeling, not a being. According to him, the duende arose during passionate moments in a musician or dancer's performance, enchanting the audience and inspiring an ecstatic group experience. Lorca believed the duende existed in the performer's soul, a sort of muse that "gives us the substance of art. . . . The duende, then, is a power, not a work."

The duende's ability to entrance people with his spells may provide the link between the fairy and flamenco music. If you've ever attended an especially enthralling concert, you know how music can elevate listeners to a seemingly enchanted state. In this case, the duende is the joy, the vitality, and the emotional power the musicians project that throws their audience into a type of mass trance. Mystical and magical rituals often use music as a tool for transcending ordinary consciousness. It's not much of a stretch, then, to envision the duende as the spirit within each of us that seeks union with the higher realms and the creative power of the universe.

When the people of the Mediterranean countries migrated to the New World, they brought their beliefs, their stories, and their fairies with them. You may see some parallels in Chapter 13: Fairies of the Americas.

"[T]he rusalka was kneeling beside Plain Kate on the deck. She was made of fog and shadow until Kate caught her eye, and then, all at once, she became human. She was young, mischievously sad, a fox in a story. Kate fell in love with her. And then she was gone."

—Erin Bow, *Plain Kate*

CHAPTER 10

Slavic Fairies

aybe it's because of the bitterly harsh winters and times of scarcity. Maybe it's because of the seemingly endless nights. Whatever the reason, many fairy tales from Russia, the Balkans, and Eastern Europe ooze doom and gloom. The fairies who appear in the folklore of these regions are more likely to drown, shred, or devour you than make your wishes come true. That's not to say they're all bad. Slavic nature spirits, like their counterparts elsewhere, are essential to our planet's survival—they take care of the plants, animals, water, and land. If you pay them respect, they may offer healing or wisdom. Legend tells us that even some of the most ferocious fairies won't harm people who have pure hearts.

"Under the general designation of fairies and fays, these spirits of the elements appear in the myth, fable, tradition, or poetry of all nations, ancient and modern. Their names are legion—peris, devs, djins, sylvans, satyrs, fauns, elves, dwarfs, trolls, norns, hisses, kobolds, brownies, and many more. They have been seen, feared, blessed, banned, and invoked in every quarter of the globe and in every age."

—Madame Helena Blavatsky, *Isis Unveiled*

The Rusalki

Among the most beguiling water spirits of Russia, Ukraine, and parts of Eastern Europe, the rusalki (singular rusalka) live in lakes, streams, and rivers during the daytime. After dark, however, they come ashore to dance and sing—and to capture men. Even guys who've heard about the dangerous shapeshifters from the time they could toddle still can't resist these gorgeous girls. Young, lusty, with full breasts and long legs, they show up as seductive as *Playboy* centerfolds and prance lewdly about in the moonlight. They even climb trees and swing among the branches like beautiful birds. Not only that, they sing like angels.

But the rusalki's heavenly appearance belies their evil intentions. Yes, they seek mates, but only briefly. Once they're done with their partners, they drown the smitten mortals without a second thought.

These bad-news babes might be a cold-hearted version of the Greek nymphs. Also akin to mermaids, at times they sport fishy tails and sit on rocks near the water, combing their lovely hair. Their enchanting voices, too, remind us of mermaids. Some folktales say the rusalki are the souls of women who drowned. Others suggest they're fertility spirits who govern the waters necessary for life. Whatever their true nature, be wary if you're out at night with your buddies and see a bunch of naked ladies emerge from a river, singing and begging for your body—they may not be what they seem.

> "Anyone who ventures near Russian rivers should protect himself against rusalki by carrying a few leaves of wormwood (*Artemisia Absinthium*) in an amulet. Wormwood also protects any article which rusalki might steal, damage, or destroy. In cases of severe infestation, one should scatter a quantity of the leaves upon the surface of the river."
>
> —Robert Ingpen and Michael Page, *Encyclopedia of Things That Never Were*

The Vila

Like the rusalki, the vila love to dance—but if you're a hunter or guilty of harming forest creatures, you don't want to be one of their partners. Forest fairies who guard the wildlife of Eastern Europe, they punish mortals who kill animals and birds without first engaging in a proper ritual of gratitude. These alluring ladies lead transgressors deep into the woods until they enter a magic circle, where the vila proceed to dance the men to death.

Also fierce protectors of women, the vila come down hard on men who betray or batter women—and woe to the man who breaks his word to a vila! But if one takes a liking to a particular guy, she may accept him as her lover. Because all vila are females, they need to mate with mortals in order to bear children. When they wish to seduce men, the vila appear as lovely young women with flowing hair, either naked or wearing shimmering, diaphanous gowns. However, these shapeshifters can also assume the forms of horses, swans, wolves, and snakes, so show special kindness to these creatures.

Fearless and formidable, the vila have been known to go into battle beside humans, if they believe the cause is just, and to provide healing to injured warriors. For this reason, some sources connect them with the Norse valkyrie.

Baba Yaga

Russian folklore portrays Baba Yaga as a cruel and bloodthirsty hag who lives in the forest and dines on children, when she can trap them. She serves as the prototype for the wicked witch in the fairy tale "Hansel and Gretel," and in "The Baba Yaga" by Aleksandr Afanasyev, she's the mean old aunt who wants to eat her niece for breakfast. In some stories she has a long, ugly nose and knives for teeth—the better to chew her victims with. Others call her "Boney Legs" because no matter how much she eats she stays as skinny as a skeleton.

Baba Yaga uses a unique form of transportation to get around the forest: a mortar and pestle, in which she can also pound herbal medicines or grind the bones of her victims. She sits in the mortar's bowl and paddles with the pestle. Swarms of nasty, shrieking spirits follow her, and wherever she goes she whips up savage winds. Even the enchanted hut where she lives behaves badly. Perched on huge chicken legs, it runs around screaming and only stops if someone utters the magic words. A fence made of bones with skulls hung on the posts surrounds the hut—an obvious deterrent to visitors. In some folktales, Baba Yaga has two older sisters and three mounted horsemen who do her bidding. She also keeps servants, including three pairs of disembodied hands. Sounds like a thoroughly disgusting and dangerous creature, right?

But early Baltic myths viewed Baba Yaga as a wise crone, Mother Time, an earth spirit who lived in the grain. A harvest/autumn divinity, she symbolized the cycle of life, death, and rebirth and guarded the Waters of Life and Death. One folk belief said that a woman who ate the last grain from the harvest, the "Baba," would give birth when springtime came. Baba Yaga also represents all that is wild and primal in nature. Like witches in general, Baba Yaga's vilification came about as a result of Christianity's growing influence in Slavic regions, when the Church revamped old deities and spirits, particularly female ones, into demons and devils in order to win the people over to a new faith.

Bird Beauties

A popular character in many Slavic fairy tales, the firebird appears as the object of a hero's quest, which leads him into unknown territory. This brilliantly colored bird isn't just an ordinary bird, of course; it's enchanted and its feathers glow with burning light. Birds often served as prophetic beings, too. In Russian folklore, three magical creatures named Sirin, Gamayun, and Alkonost have beautiful women's heads, feathered bodies, and exquisite voices. The paintings of Viktor Vasnetsov, Sergey Solomko, Anastasia Melnikova, Elena Flerova, and other artists show you what they look like (see *www.viola.bz/sirin* to view some images). Given fairies' propensity for shapeshifting, perhaps they're related.

The Tündér

Tündér means "fairy" in Hungarian, and unlike the other ladies we've talked about in this chapter, they're both beautiful and benevolent. Some of these nature spirits live in magnificent castles high in the mountains, others in palaces filled with jewels beneath lakes or on islands surrounded by lush gardens. Humanlike in form, they can shapeshift into animals, birds, fish, or trees—or make themselves invisible. The tündér possess unlimited wealth because all their body fluids are magical and can generate gems and precious metals. When they cry, their tears turn to pearls and, according to Hungarian storyteller Zalka Csenge Virág, "when fairies pee in the water, their pee turns into gold." It's said that these generous beings give pearls to poor people and orphans.

Sometimes the tündér marry mortal men, as did the most famous of these fairies, Ilona. In the story "Prince Argyilus and the Fairy Ilona," a prince falls in love with the fairy queen. One night Argyilus notices fairies, who've shapeshifted into ravens, stealing golden

apples from a magical tree in his father's garden and decides to climb that tree in an attempt to find the fairy he loves. Reminiscent of the Tree of Life or the Celtic World Tree, it reaches high into the heavens. But when the prince asks the sun, moon, and winds about Ilona, they can't help him. Next, the prince asks the forest creatures where he might find the fairy, and a lame wolf explains that a wicked witch locked her away in a castle. À la "Sleeping Beauty," the witch cast a spell on Ilona, putting her into a deep sleep—only the prince can wake her with a kiss. After staying awake by the fairy's side for three days and nights, he gets his chance and kisses Ilona, breaking the spell and turning the tables on the witch.

In *Hungarian and Vogul Mythology*, Géza Róheim tells us that the fairy queen Ilona appeared as a swan swimming in the Danube and links her with the swan goddess revered in pre-Christian Hungary. This powerful, supernatural being could appear or disappear at will and cause other things to appear and disappear, too. In Transylvania, people call the Milky Way "the Fairy's Way."

Flowers or Fairies?

According to a fairy tale recounted by Hungarian storyteller Zalka Csenge Virág, water lilies evolved from a young fairy named Rózsa. The fairy queen, Ilona, turned the girl into a flower so that after all the fairies were gone, she could still keep watch over the human world. Hungarians call water lilies "fairy roses."

Other Fascinating Fairies

Because few people could read or write in what is now eastern Poland, Western Russia, Belorussia, and Ukraine until after Christianity took hold there, we have to rely on oral tradition, songs, and fairy tales to learn about the supernatural beings who populated these areas in the early days. During those times, when dense forests covered much of the land and people's lives were closely entwined with nature, it seems logical that a host of nature spirits would have dwelt among the Slavic mortals. Let's meet a few of them now.

THE BEREGINY

The oldest of the Slavic spirits, the Bereginy are the ancestors of the rusalki. They live in the forests, lakes, and rivers, but you're most likely to find them in liminal zones, where land and water meet: beaches, rocky shores, riverbanks, and marshes. Presided over by the goddess Beregina, whose name means "earth" and "shore," these water spirits bear similarities to both the Greek nymphae and mermaids. Sometimes they appear as twin-tailed mermaids or fertility divinities. In the old days, women honored the Bereginy with outdoor rituals, but when Christianity labeled the spirits "demons," legends say the women retreated to the bathhouses to meet with the fairies in secret. There the Bereginy became associated with the goddesses of fate, known as the Rozhanitsy.

THE LESHACHIKHA

Les means "forest" in some Slavic languages. Legend says these forest fairies were the wives of the woods deities known as the leshy and the mothers of the leshonki. As protectors of the forests and their inhabitants, they guarded their territory diligently—anyone who entered with bad intent or who harmed nature's creatures were led by the leshachikha deep into the woods where the mortals might never again see the light of day. These nature spirits can appear as animals or leaves, and they supposedly "die" in autumn, when the earth in northern climes shifts into its dormant phase. When spring comes again, the leshachikha arise, reborn after their long winter's nap. If you fear these spirits might cast a spell on you, stand under a tree and take off all your clothes, then put them on again backward.

THE LAUMÉS

Fairy spinners and weavers who work long into the wee hours of the night, the laumés bear some similarities to the Greek Fates. Early folklore describes them as beautiful females with long, flowing hair who protected orphans and aided the poor. Like other nature fairies, they make their homes deep in the woods, rivers, and other remote places. However, some myths say these spirits live in the clouds, and whenever you see a rainbow you know they hung it there. Their dancing and singing bring rain, sleet, hail, and snow. By the seventeenth century, however, witchcraft hysteria in Europe cast them in a more negative light as shapeshifting hags who changed themselves and humans into toads. Today the word *lauma* means "hag" and *lauminette* means "to practice witchcraft."

THE DEIVES

Conflicting reports exist about the appearance of these ancient Lithuanian spirits. Some sources describe them as frightful old hags with two faces. Others say they're buxom, blue-eyed blonde beauties. Like other fairies, they can shapeshift into animals, particularly horses, bears, and goats. Regardless of their looks, the deives are a generous and compassionate lot, repelled by greed and selfishness. They also guard and guide women and show sympathy for their work conditions—sort of a supernatural Occupational Safety and Health Administration. Folklore says they forbid spinning on Thursdays and washing laundry after sunset (apparently because the deives like to swim in the dark and don't want to be disturbed by mortals). In some

legends, they occupy a place similar to the Greek Fates as seven spinning and weaving sisters who determine human destiny.

THE KESHALYI

Some folklore describes these fairies as spinners and weavers similar to the Greek Fates. Reported to inhabit the forests and mountains of Transylvania, these lovely ladies are the children of a very fertile fairy queen named Ana. Consequently, Slavic people petition them to help with fertility problems. The problem is, each of Ana's offspring came into the world with a disease, perhaps because her husband, Locolita, wasn't exactly a nice guy. According to legend, Ana initially rejected the advances of this evil king but eventually succumbed for the good of her fairy subjects. Part of the bargain stated that when one of the keshalyi reached the age of 999, she must marry one of Locolita's men.

A fine line exists between Slavic fairies and deities, for in the early myths many of the characters intermingled. Additionally, some supernatural beings who once held positions as gods and goddesses became reduced to fairies over time. Today, Slavic fairy tales provide anthropologists with insight into the ancient religious beliefs and customs of the people who've occupied these regions for millennia. In fact, given the dearth of written records, fairy tales may be the only true source of information.

"The people of Asia, Arabia, and Persia told [fairy tales] in their own way, not for children, but for grown-up people. There were no novels then, nor any printed books, of course; but there were people whose profession it was to amuse men and women by telling tales."

—Muhsin Mahdi, *The Arabian Nights*

CHAPTER 11

African, Persian, and Middle Eastern Fairies

xotic and enchanting, the ancient lands of the Middle East, Mesopotamia, Persia, and Northern Africa gave birth to some of the world's greatest artistic and literary treasures. More than 2,500 years ago, a great library in Alexandria, Egypt, housed much of the world's literature, and nearly 4,000 years ago the Great Sphinx emerged from the Giza desert as a larger-than-life testament that supernatural beings shared the earth with humans. Many of our religious roots and fervently held beliefs also come from these lands. Although Westerners might not connect fairies and fairy tales with these regions, if you delve into the rich body of folklore from Africa and the Middle East, you'll find surprising legends of mystical beings and many fascinating avenues worth wandering down in your search for the fey.

The Thousand and One Nights

The most famous collection of tales from the Middle East, *The Thousand and One Nights*, a.k.a. the *Arabian Nights*, is also one of the oldest. Although its exact origins are shrouded in mystery, the earliest known Arabic version appears to have been written in the eighth century. Since then, many other translations and variations have turned up, composed by numerous authors over an extended period of time. The *Nights* contains 1,000 stories plus a frame tale. The stories are drawn from many sources and many lands, including Egypt, Turkey, Iran, Iraq, and India, and they include lots of supernatural beings.

In the backstory, the wife of a king named Shahryar betrays him, and he harbors so much bitterness toward women that he marries and then kills a different one every day—3,000 in all. Naturally, terror reigns in his kingdom. When the king's vizier marries his own daughter, the clever Scheherazade, to the bloodthirsty king, not only do the murders end, but a rich body of stories emerges. Each night, the delightful storyteller Scheherazade entertains the king with a bedtime story of magic and mystery, leaving off the ending so he must tune in again tomorrow for the conclusion—and, therefore, allow her to live another day. This goes on for 1,000 nights, during which the king falls in love with Scheherazade and calls off her execution.

A favorite tale in the West, "Aladdin and the Wonderful Lamp," features two magical beings known as genies or jinn. The young Aladdin summons one jinni by rubbing a magic ring, and the other, more powerful spirit by rubbing a magic oil lamp in which the jinni has been trapped for a long, long time. Once released from the lamp, the jinni—a gift-giving type of fairy—must do whatever Aladdin asks.

The theme of a magical being confined in a container seems unique to tales from this part of the world. According to legend, King Solomon imprisoned the evil and rebellious jinn who opposed him in bottles, flasks, and other containers. But even though the rules say a jinni has to serve whoever frees him, he's not always happy about it and may put up a fight—even threaten his liberator's life—before granting any wishes.

The Jinn

Also spelled djinn (singular jinni), these male and female spirits from Arabic mythology occupy lower rungs on the spiritual ladder than angels or devils and hover somewhere beyond humans. They also share characteristics with Western fairies. Like fairies elsewhere, some jinn treat mortals decently and even present them with gifts; others endanger people or at least disrupt their lives. When they take a dislike to particular humans, the jinn punish them with illnesses or injuries, and mythology blames the fairies for causing all kinds of accidents. Even the supposedly benevolent jinn can't be trusted, for like most fairies they're notoriously unreliable.

Fairy Sightings
· · · · · · · · · · · · · · · · · · · ·

Ibn al-Athir, an Arabic historian of Islamic tradition, noted that a devastating throat disease plagued the city of Mosul on the Tigris River in the year 600 of the Hijra calendar (about c.e. 1200). A female jinn grieving her dead son supposedly conjured the disease and infected anyone who didn't console her.

Some sources say these spirits of flame can live just about anywhere: underground, in trees or stones, in rivers or marketplaces, in the air or in fire. Arabic tales say they resided on earth thousands of years before Adam and Eve. Others claim the jinn make their home in the mystical mountains of Kaf, in a region called Jinnestan. Made of green chrysolite, these mountains stand 2,000 miles high and ring the earth.

Folklore tells us that the jinn crave many of the things humans do, including food and drink, and that, like mortals, they can be killed by other fairies or humans, unlike some mythical creatures who appear to be immortal. However, they're not limited by the same physical restrictions as people—they can shapeshift into animal or human forms, for instance, or make themselves invisible. Instead of blood, fire flows through their veins, and they spontaneously combust when dealt a fatal blow. In Egypt, female jinn look and act a lot like the Greek sirens: They dwell in the waterways of the Nile, sing like angels, and drown men who happen to fall under their spells.

In Muslim ideology, people who die in sin may transition into jinn for a period of time after death. Islamic belief also states that the jinn have free will. Marriages between the jinn and mortals apparently took place in the past, with some degree of success.

Cyber-Jinn

Centuries ago, the jinn served as muses to poets and artists and shared secrets about the future with fortunetellers. Today, according to G. Willow Wilson in *Alif, the Unseen*, they stir up all sorts of technological nightmares in the modern world. If your computer has ever malfunctioned for no apparent reason or your e-mail has been hacked into, perhaps you should blame the jinn. Wilson classifies the jinn—both ancient and contemporary—into five categories.

MARID

Remember that dynamic and imposing jinni in the story of Aladdin? Most likely he's a marid, a powerful male spirit with a commanding voice and a no-nonsense attitude. These spirits can get into your flash drive and totally mess up your operating system.

EFFRIT

Smarter than your average jinn, effrit live in caves or underground. Mischievous and capricious, these beings can shift from good to bad or bad to good. In the Qur'an, it's said that the effrit took orders from King Solomon and acted as his servants. Today, these schemers invade your privacy, send phony Facebook messages, and can even write computer code.

GHOULS

In the West, we think of ghouls as the undead, zombies who prey on people. That's pretty much how they appear in Islamic stories, too. Dumber than dirt and unrelentingly evil, they roam around cemeteries at night and have absolutely no concern for human well-being—they even nosh on human flesh when they can get it. They don't pose much of a threat in the technological realm, though, simply because they're too ignorant.

SILA

These intelligent ladies get along better with humans than many jinn and rarely intend to harm mortals or interfere with their lives. Clever shapeshifters, they easily transcend the boundaries between the races. But even though they may not mean to cause trouble, their meddlesome nature can still be annoying.

VETALA

These vampire-like entities can assume human bodies and trick people into believing they really are mortals. Of course, you can't trust them—and what's more, they can shapeshift into other forms so you don't have a clue whom you're dealing with. They also like to lure you into mind games that can derail you from more important activities.

At *www.aliftheunseen.com,* Wilson says that IT specialists are trying to understand and control the online jinn and to guard mortals against their nefarious behavior. At this time, however, the jinn's power remains uncurbed, and risks to computers and their operators still exist. If you fear attacks by cyber-jinn, Wilson recommends stepping away from your computer and calling your IT professional.

Persia's Peri

In the mythology of ancient Persia, a light being named Ormuzd presided in the heavens, accompanied by six amshaspands, twenty-eight izeds, and a host of less important entities called ferohers. An opposing power known as Aherman reigned in the dark kingdom, with six arch-deevs and a whole lot of lesser deevs. As humans in this volatile part of the world have done for millennia, these supernatural beings warred among themselves constantly.

The Persian fairies known as peris and deevs evolved from this early system, although the myths about them now include a huge helping of Islamic belief mixed in. And to this day, the fairies are still fighting. According to some sources, the peris live in Jinnestan, along with the jinn and the deevs. The various fairies occupy separate kingdoms, each comprising numerous provinces and cities. In the peri-province Shad-u-kâm, which means "pleasure and delight," sit the capital city of Juherabâd (the jewel city) and the beautiful Amberabâd (the amber city)—places glowing with gems and magnificent castles. Interestingly, the peris don't eat; they subsist entirely on the scents from perfume—which, not incidentally, repel their enemies, the deevs. When the evil deevs succeed in capturing peri prisoners, they lock the fairies in cages and hang them from the tops of tall trees; their peri pals bring the captives delicious aromas to inhale.

In their battles against the bigger and meaner deevs, the peris sometimes enlist the aid of mortals, the most famous being a warrior named Tahmuras. The fairies bolstered him with magic spells and talismans and gave him a multilingual talking bird who could see the future as his guide. She transported Tahmuras to Jinnestan, where ordinarily humans can't go. There the hero did what heroes do—he destroyed some cruel deevs, rescued a kidnapped maiden, but ultimately perished. Another human deev-slayer, Roostem, picked up where Tahmuras left off, hunting and killing the peris' enemies, ad infinitum. Search and destroy is the stuff of which Persian fairy tales are made.

How would you recognize these fairies if you encountered them? Thomas Keightley in his book *The Fairy Mythology* describes the leader of the deevs as impossible to miss—he stands about 230 feet tall and about twenty-eight feet wide, with a black face, a hair-covered body, boar's tusks, bloody pools for eyes, and hair like needles and snakes where pigeons roost. However, Keightley calls the Peri "the fairest creation of poetical imagination." Exquisitely beautiful ephemeral beings made of fire and light, these humanlike fairies seem to radiate colored light and bear similarities to angels. Sometimes peris shapeshift into birds and on occasion mate with mortals. A Persian man can offer a woman no higher compliment than to compare her to a peri.

"But hark!—I hear Zuleika's voice;
Like Houris' hymn it meets mine ear:
She is the offspring of my choice;
Oh! more than ev'n her mother dear,
With all to hope, and nought to fear
My Peri!—ever welcome here!
Sweet, as the desert fountain's wave,
To lips just cool'd in time to save
Such to my longing sight art thou;
Nor can they waft to Mecca's shrine
More thanks for life, than I for thine,
Who blest thy birth, and bless thee now."

—Lord Byron, "The Bride of Abydos"

The Seven Hathors

In ancient Egypt, the goddess Hathor governed love, sex, pleasure, the arts, music, dancing, perfume, alcohol, and all the sensual joys of life. No wonder she was so popular. She sometimes appeared wearing a cow's horns with a disc held between them, which represented the sun, but she also shapeshifted into a lioness, falcon, snake, or a hippopotamus when it pleased her.

Mythology says she expressed herself as seven spirits known as "the Seven Hathors," but here things get a little confusing. Some sources describe these spirits as aspects of the goddess; others refer to them as her children or assistants. Early Egyptian art often portrays the Hathors as beautiful women playing tambourines and wearing the goddess's horns-and-disc headdress, though they sometimes appear as cows.

The Seven Hathors resemble the Fates of ancient Greece. These fortune-telling spirits knew everyone's destiny and the fate of the nation. They appeared at a child's birth to reveal the baby's future and time of death. They also followed the souls of deceased people into the afterlife. According to Ancient Egypt Online (*www.ancientegyptonline.co.uk*) "the 'Seven Hathors' were worshiped in seven cities: Waset (Thebes), Iunu (On, Heliopolis), Aphroditopolis, Sinai, Momemphis, Herakleopolis, and Keset." Myths also connect them with the star cluster known as the Pleiades or the Seven Sisters.

Africa's Yumboes

The people of West Africa speak of a race of fairies known as the yumboes, though out of respect they call the fairies *Bakhna Rakhna*, or Good People—much as the Irish and British do to avert fey mischief. About two feet in height with silver hair and pearly white bodies, the yumboes live in luxurious underground dwellings located in the Paps hills. There, mysterious disembodied hands and feet serve the yumboes and their guests at lavishly laid banquet tables.

But in the evenings, the yumboes enter the mortal world, where they filch corn and couscous from people's kitchens. They also fish at night, then steal fire from humans—but only as much as they need to cook their food. It seems that the yumboes, like the British brownies, connect themselves with certain families. Some sources say the fairies are the spirits of deceased relatives, and when a family member dies, the yumboes mourn and dance on the departed person's grave.

Fairy Sightings

When a German/Baltic botanist and explorer named Georg Schweinfurth found pygmies living in central Africa in the 1870s, his discovery seemed to provide proof that fairies had, in fact, existed since prehistoric times. Colonel R.G. Haliburton, a Canadian, believed his explorations had turned up a race of Akka dwarfs in Morocco. The so-called "pygmy theory" suggested that these diminutive folk had inspired concepts of the British brownies and other fairies. In his scholarly paper *Dwarf Survivals and Traditions* (1895), Haliburton described the pygmies as "little dark-complexioned smiths and magicians" and thought that at one time they had inhabited the entire planet.

Other Fairy Folk of Africa and the Middle East

You'd expect to find a wide array of fairies in these ancient and diverse cultures, and indeed, many unusual spirits do show up in the myths and legends of Africa and the Middle East. In addition to the most prominent ones that we've already discussed, here are some other supernatural beings with colorful characteristics.

THE ABATWA

These miniature fairies look like humans, except they're only about half an inch in size. They live in the southern part of Africa, in anthills they share with the resident ants. Legend says these shy, reclusive beings only let children and pregnant women—or people with magical knowledge—see them, perhaps riding on the backs of ants. They hunt with poisoned arrows and reportedly get angry if you comment upon their size. The Abatwa are also a race of pygmies from Africa's Great Lakes region.

THE TOKOLOSH

Another South African fairy called the tokolosh (or tokoloshi, tikoloshe, tikoloshi) looks like a dark, hairy male dwarf. A water spirit in times past, he now serves as a domestic helper to witches and wizards. When these spirits want to become invisible, they place magic pebbles in their mouths and vanish. Some tales say that female witches inherit the tokolosh from their mothers and keep them as lovers. Mischievous beings known for stealing milk from cows, tokoloshes can be trapped by sprinkling around a concoction made from a dead tokolosh.

THE EKIMMU

The ancient Assyrians and Sumerians spoke of a vengeful spirit called an ekimmu, who prophesied death by shrieking like an Irish banshee near the home of a person who's about to pass over. These creepy, vampire-like spirits also sucked life from sleeping and unsuspecting humans and supposedly plagued humans with disease and unlawful desires.

THE DIBBUK

A demon in Jewish mythology, the dibbuk got its name during the seventeenth century from German and Polish Jews. Before that, Talmudic literature mentioned it only as an evil or unclean spirit. Dibbukim can possess humans and cause insanity. According to the *Encyclopaedia Judaica*, the dibbuk was originally considered a devil that attached itself to the bodies of people who were ill. Another belief says the dibbuk enters a living person who has committed a sin that "opened a door" for the demon to take over. Still other sources suggest they're the spirits of dead people who, for various reasons, were never laid to rest. Tales dating from about 500 B.C.E. through the first century C.E. speak of these evil beings, though by the Renaissance they'd apparently lost much of their caché.

MAZIKEEN

These Jewish fairies, a.k.a. the shideem or shehireem, came into being after Adam and Eve got thrown out of the Garden of Eden. For 130 years, Adam and Eve were separated, during which time Adam mated with female spirits and Eve with males, producing offspring known as the mazikeen. Hebrew mythology describes them as tiny, elf-like beings. Other sources liken them to the Arabic jinn. These spirits exhibit traits common to other fairies—they sport wings and fly, they can change shape and appear as other creatures, and they possess the gift of prophecy. Like fairies in other lands, they also enjoy revelry, food, and drink. But unlike some supernatural beings, the mazikeen aren't immortal.

A modern-day character named Mazikeen appears in the comic book series *Lucifer* as the lover of Lucifer Morningstar, a descendant of Lilith, Adam's first wife. She also shows up in Neil Gaiman's *Sandman* series.

Fairies from the Middle Eastern and African regions have survived for countless generations—and coming from the Cradle of Civilization, they may perch in all of our family trees. Certainly these spirits show no signs of relinquishing their allure or their influence on creative minds in the modern day. In addition to the 1992 animated film *Aladdin*, Disney has spawned an array of games based on Aladdin's adventures. The jinn show up as fearsome fellows in contemporary fantasy games. You can even buy peri-doll necklaces and peri chopsticks on eBay.

"On a gold throne, whose radiating brightness

Dazzles the eyes—enhaloing the scene;

Sits a fair form, arrayed in snowy whiteness,

She is Chang-o, the beauteous Fairy Queen.

"Rainbow-winged angels softly hover o'er her,

Forming a canopy above the throne;

A host of fairy beings stand before her,

Each robed in light and girt with meteor zone."

—George Carter Stent,
The Jade Chaplet in Twenty-Four Beads

CHAPTER 12

ℐairies of Asia
and Australia

ike fairy tales in all cultures, Asian stories reflect the society in which they arose and teach the mores of the social order. Chinese fairy tales, for instance, speak of clan structure, the family as a sociopolitical unit, the importance of duty over personal interests, respect for ancestors, and obedience to authority. Some Chinese and Japanese stories also provide insight into real-life events, rulers, places, art, and architecture, making them good sources for historical study. In many Asian fairy tales enchanted animals and trees play prominent roles, along with magicians, sages, demons, and deities. In Indian fairy tales, even words have magical power—they can assume various forms and shape people. Stories, it's said, exist in the ethers—not in the imagination of storytellers—and it's up to people to discover and tell the tales. Stories are gifts and must circulate. By listening to a tale—really listening—you become transformed. "If you know a tale," explains A.K. Ramanujan in *Folktales from India*, "you owe it not only to others but to the tale itself to tell it; otherwise it suffocates."

The Gift of Immortality

Fairies enjoy immortality, or at least exceptional longevity—something we humans have sought ever since we first set foot on earth. If you want to live forever, one way is to befriend the fairies who make their home on China's mystical mountain Kw'en Lun, for here grows *k'iung shu*, the Tree of Life. A tree of truly majestic proportions, it stands 15,000 feet high—ten times as tall as the Empire State Building—and its trunk measures 1,800 feet around. This ancient and venerable tree only bears fruit (sometimes described as peaches) once every 3,000 years—and only the fairies can pick it. If the fairies really like you, they might give you a piece of the magic fruit to eat, and *voila*, you're immortal, too!

That's not the only fairy recipe for immortality, however. Kw'en Lun's fairies also grow coriander and sesamum, then eat the seeds. However, chewing ordinary coriander and sesame seeds from your local supermarket might not do the trick. You could try blending gum from a peach tree with powdered mulberries, crushed cinnabar, and liquid (colloidal) gold—but you'll still need a fairy to add a drop of magic to the mixture to get it to work.

How can you get to fairyland? Legend says you cross the Azure Bridge into the Jasper City. There you'll find Yao chi, the Jasper Lake, a magnificent (and undoubtedly magical) body of water. One Chinese story tells of two men who came upon a lovely bridge in the mountains. Two beautiful young women met them there and invited the mortals to walk with them over the bridge, into the realm of the fairies. The men enjoyed a pleasant visit—possibly lunch or dinner—with their delightful companions, and then decided to return home. But when they arrived back in the human world, they discovered seven generations had passed since they first met the fairies on the bridge.

Fairy Mother Si-wang-mu

The queen of the fairies, Si-wang-mu, seated high on her mountain, has an ideal vantage point from which to observe the behavior of mortals. When she spots people doing things she finds objectionable, she wastes no time in raining punishments down on them. She also has the power to confer immortality on humans, but she's pretty particular about whom she favors with that gift. Legend says the Emperor Mu asked for her secret recipe for the elixir of youth, but she remained as tight-lipped as a celebrity chef. She did agree to a compromise, however, and gave the emperor seven peaches he could plant to grow his own Tree of Life. What she didn't tell him was that they wouldn't grow on earth.

"Emperor Liang when tired fell asleep in the sunshine and dreamed that he was visited by a woman of celestial beauty. He asked whence she came and who she was. 'I live on the terrace of the Sun on the Enchanted Mountain. In the morning I am a cloud, in the evening a shower of rain.' "

 —University of Oregon Libraries

Star-Crossed Lovers

Like fairies everywhere, Chinese spirits sometimes marry mortals, though their families rarely approve. One ancient story called "The Fairy Couple" or "The Cowherd and the Weaver Girl" tells the tale of two star-crossed lovers, whom the Qi Xi Festival commemorates on the seventh day of the seventh month of the Chinese calendar. The popular tale has many variations and has been interpreted in films, TV shows, and dramatic productions. In one version, the stars Vega (the Weaver Girl Star) and Altair (the Cowherd Star) fall in love— a travesty, because deities in Chinese mythology aren't supposed to engage in romantic affairs. When the Empress of the Heavens, the girl's grandmother, finds out, she banishes the cowherd to earth and sentences the girl to an eternity of weaving clouds.

On earth, the cowherd endures a hardscrabble life for many years with only an old ox as a companion. By plowing fields, he manages

to eke out a living. What he doesn't realize, though, is that the ox is an enchanted animal, previously the Gold Ox Star.

One day, the fairies ask the empress to let them visit earth to bathe in a magical lake, known for its salubrious properties, and they want to take the weaver girl with them. The empress decides her granddaughter deserves a break and allows the group to go. When the ox learns about the girls bathing naked in the lake, he tells the cowherd to snatch a red dress lying on the shore.

The young man does, but he frightens the rest of the fairies, who grab their clothes and fly back to their home in the sky, leaving the weaver girl behind.

The cowherd offers to return the dress if the girl will marry him. Recognizing him as her former sweetheart, she agrees and the couple have two children. For a while, they live a simple but happy life together on earth. When the old ox finally dies, they strip off his hide and preserve it, for the ox had promised that one day the cowherd could make a cloak from it and fly back to the heavens.

Meanwhile, the empress has been fuming over her granddaughter's disobedience and sends soldiers to bring her home. As the fairy army flies away with its captive, the cowherd dons the magic cloak, grabs their two children, and flies after the soldiers. The empress, however, has no intentions of letting the pair be together. Using her hairpin, she scratches a barrier of stars—the Milky Way—between the lovers to keep them apart. The family cries; the fairies cry; the deities cry. Finally, the empress relents and allows the weaver girl and the cowherd to meet once a year on the seventh day of the seventh month. So they can reach each other, flocks of magpies spread their wings to form a bridge in the sky for the family to cross.

Why the Chinese Began Using Firecrackers

Legend says tiny, humanlike fairies, only about a foot tall, live in China's western hills. If provoked, they cause mortals to suffer with awful fevers and chills. To frighten these fairies away, the people began burning bamboo fires. Later, when the Chinese developed firecrackers, they used those instead to ward off the malevolent spirits.

Japan's Kappa

Not all fairies dazzle us with their beauty. In fact, some are hideous creatures, and the Japanese kappa falls into that category. This grotesque water-goblin—who's been around for ages but didn't really gain popularity until the Edo period (1615–1868)—also has some peculiar kinks that we don't see in fairies elsewhere, thankfully. For instance, the lecherous kappa likes to hide out in public restrooms where he can fondle the buttocks of unsuspecting women. Japanese legends describe these water spirits as being about three to four feet tall with chartreuse skin, webbed feet, and fish scales or turtle shells covering their bodies. The kappa's strangest feature, however, is a bowl-like hollow on the top of his head that holds a magical liquid—the source of his strength. If you can trick him into spilling that liquid—by bowing, for example—he forfeits his powers.

Folklore often describes the kappa as flesh-eating spirits that live in rivers and lakes. Some tales liken them to vampires—supposedly they attack livestock, drag the beasts into water and drown them, and then suck out their life essence and/or eat their livers. Other sources say the kappa can even shapeshift into a type of bacteria that purifies sewer water, so these creepy guys aren't all bad. And if you manage to capture a kappa, you can force it to reveal its knowledge of bonesetting and other healing practices.

But here's the oddest thing about the kappa. According to legend, every human has a small ball called a *shirikodama* nestled in the intestines, which some sources say is the person's soul. Others connect it with the liver—the kappa's favorite food. For whatever reason—no one seems to know exactly why—the kappa want the shirikodama and kill mortals in order to obtain this magic ball.

As is true of fairies and other supernatural creatures in general, modern media has cleaned up the kappa. Contemporary cartoons por-

tray him as weird-looking, but almost cute. You can even buy baseball-playing kappa dolls, kappa refrigerator magnets, and kappa toothpicks to put in your child's lunchbox. Of course, nobody these days alludes to his vicious or kinky behavior, but you might want to think twice about letting your kids hang out with a kappa . . .

The Fairy-Fox

The word *kitsune* means "fox" in Japanese, but in mythology it means so much more. The fairy kitsune, like the Native American coyote, is a magical trickster who symbolizes the concepts of metamorphosis and transformation. This supernatural being lives as a white fox for 100 years, after which it can assume human form. During that time, it grows nine furry tails (nine being a number of transition and transformation), and the only way to kill a kitsune is to cut off all nine tails. Sometimes this spirit takes the shape of a beautiful woman or occasionally an older man—but the kitsune always appears in folklore as a wise, magical, and mischievous being.

Legend breaks down the mysterious fox-spirit into three basic categories: the zenko or "good" kitsune, the yako or malevolent fox, and the ninko, who usually remains invisible to humans. Many more types of kitsune exist, but all have one thing in common: They can't be caged. Freedom is essential to their well-being.

Like all fairy beings, the kitsune possesses magical powers, including the abilities to alter time and to make itself invisible—it can also shapeshift into the moon, a tree, a vampire, a human, etc. The kitsune enjoys playing pranks on mortals, especially wealthy, prominent, and boastful people. Tricksters and illusionists, they create scenarios and environments that completely confuse mortals so that the hapless humans can't possibly decipher "reality" from "fantasy." In typical

fairy tradition, the foxes may lead people (usually men) astray until they're entirely lost and befuddled, whether in the forest or the Tokyo Metro. The kitsune might also steal possessions, seduce, humiliate, or seek vengeance on humans.

According to an old tale, you shouldn't go outdoors if the sun shines *and* it's raining—that's when the kitsune get married, and you don't want to disturb their festivities. This peculiar weather phenomenon is called kitsune-bi, meaning foxfire. Some people believe it signals good fortune, a sign of fertility that enhances crop growth. It's also considered an optimal time for humans to marry.

Magic Birds

If you've ever studied Japanese art, you've no doubt noticed the prevalence of birds in paintings, ceramics, and fabrics. Birds carry special significance in Japanese mythology—especially the crane or tsuru, which symbolizes good fortune, longevity, and fidelity. Consequently, they appear in many legends and stories. Fairies known as the yosei frequently show up as cranes, swans, or other birds.

A birdlike spirit called the tengu figures prominently in Japanese folklore and fairy tales. This creature sometimes shows up as a human-bird composite and sometimes as a humanlike being with either a long nose or a beak. Like birds, the tengu live in trees—they even hatch from eggs.

Often considered wilderness spirits, they protect the forests as other nature fairies do. If you don't want to anger the tengu, be sure to make offerings to trees or other plants before cutting them down. Capricious, as most fairies are, the tengu may aid or harm mortals for no discernable reason. Legends say they can take possession of

humans and drive them insane. The tengu also lead people into the wilderness, from which they never return. They're even rumored to eat mortals—and if they zap you with their magic bamboo wands, you'll spontaneously combust!

Origami Cranes

Origami, the Japanese art of paper folding, dates back four centuries. Delicate origami cranes, however, are more than beautiful—they represent healing and peace. After World War II, a woman named Sadako Sasaki, who came down with leukemia after being exposed to radiation at Hiroshima, hoped to tap the magic healing properties of the tsuru by folding 1,000 paper cranes. Since then, people seeking peace have carried on her legacy by sending origami cranes to the Hiroshima memorial. The staff of the Japanese American National Museum, along with many other people, brought this lovely tradition to New York after 9/11, folding thousands of cranes to distribute throughout the city.

Nāgás and Nāginis

These powerful water spirits embody the dual themes of creation-destruction exemplified in so many fairies. Considered minor nature deities in Vedic tradition, they're believed to be the ancestors of humans—even some of India's most prominent families. Usually depicted with human torsos and snaky lower parts, they can also be thought of as a type of mermaid—except for one unique feature: seven or more cobra-hooded heads. Even so, mythology describes them as extremely handsome creatures, especially the females.

The nāgás (males) and nāginīs (females) make their homes beneath lakes and rivers, where they live in elegant palaces. There, they guard treasure—both material and spiritual. According to legend, these protector spirits also oversee the waters of the world and are responsible for weather conditions involving water: rain, floods, and typhoons. They bite people who harm the environment and may even kill them, but if the nāgás and nāginīs like you they'll share sacred wisdom with you.

Nagaland

In his book *Nagaland: A Journey to India's Forgotten Frontier* (2011), British journalist Jonathan Glancey takes readers to

> *"a forgotten corner of the world. It isn't at all well known even in India, and it is much misunderstood. I had known about the Naga hills from childhood. For me, at that stage of life, and as someone with a great love for India, this was a Secret Garden or Lost Kingdom, a land from a Kipling story. As I grew up, I remained curious. When I finally went to Nagaland in the early 1980s, I had the opportunity—not as a journalist— to tell the story of a people and a place that deserve recognition. I have been astonished by how little people in India know about Nagaland and its extraordinary history. Here, aside from a fascinating people with a rich culture, is a land that has been a junction box for political ambitions that have shaped the world. This is where the Japanese nearly invaded India in 1944. This is where China might have invaded in 1962. For any number of reasons, Nagaland matters."*

Other Fairies from Hindu and Buddhist Mythology

Many more colorful, supernatural beings populate these ancient and rich bodies of mythology—too many to cover here. Some bear similarities to fairies in other parts of the world and some have their own unique qualities and characteristics. India's mystical ideas influenced folklore and fairy beliefs in other parts of Asia, too. Here are some supernatural beings you might find interesting.

THE DEVAS

Buddhism adopted the spirits known as devas from Hinduism. The word *deva* means "shining one." Different classes of devas exist, from nature spirits to transcendent beings who occupy a blissful realm beyond anything mortals can imagine. Some devas even have human-like shapes, and legend tells us that once upon a time humans could do many of the things the devas can do, including flying and glowing with heavenly light. Although devas enjoy long lifetimes—thousands of years or more—they aren't immortal. Nor do they usually interact with humans, except perhaps to offer gentle insight or guidance. Today, we generally think of devas as nature fairies.

THE ASURAS

Usually considered powerful demons, these spirits were the enemies of the devas. Numerous asuras exist in Hindu mythology, often portrayed as giants or huge, evil creatures who warred with the gods. Some stories say they descended from the same father, the asuras siding with evil, the devas siding with good.

THE DAKINIS

This female air spirit's name translates as "cloud fairy," "celestial woman," "sky dancer," and "space-goer." In Tibetan Buddhism, *dakini* also connotes emptiness, and some sources describe dakinis as embodiments or emanations of Enlightened Mind. They may serve as ethereal guardians to mortals, much like angels. Some stories link them with death and say they inhabit places such as cemeteries, cremation byres, and battlefields. As spiritual messengers, they bring wisdom to humankind and initiate mortals into the ancient mysteries. Human women who exemplify compassion and realization may also be called dakinis.

THE MUMIAI

It seems that these mean-spirited fairies don't much like the lower castes in India, for they most often show up in poor communities to hand down justice and punishment. Thieves and other wrongdoers reap the worst of the mumiai's vengeance—the fairies might destroy everything offending mortals own, ruin their crops, even drive them away from their homes.

THE RAKSHASAS

These ugly goblins from Hindu legend have bulls' heads, tusks, and huge stomachs. However, they can also shapeshift into beautiful women when they want to trap men to eat for dinner. These nasty demons get blamed for causing leprosy, but they sometimes put their medical knowledge to good use by raising the dead and reattaching lost body parts.

THE VIRIKAS

Tiny beings (eighteen inches tall or even shorter) with red bodies, these death spirits appear at the homes of people who are about to die—like the Irish bean sidhe. Their bloody teeth suggest they might try to eat the deceased, so to appease them people offer them gifts of rice, spices, and red cloth.

THE YAKSHAS AND YAKSHINIS

Nature spirits in both Hinduism and Buddhism, these gentle fairies protect earth's natural resources. They reside in lakes, wells, forests, mountains, even cities. Legend says they hide treasure at the bottom of trees and guard it. Their leader, Kubera, rules from a place called Alaka, a fairy kingdom hidden high in the Himalayas.

Fairies Down Under

As people from Europe and other countries immigrated to Australia and New Zealand, they brought their fairy tales with them. These stories mingled with the native Aboriginal folklore to form a large, diverse pantheon of spirits and deities—creator and destroyer beings,

nature fairies, trickster types, animal hybrids, sky and ocean spirits, even one called Barraiya who supposedly fashioned the first vagina. Some people say the fairies migrated Down Under to enjoy better lives once Europe became too industrialized. By the beginning of the twentieth century, fairy lore in these parts had become so popular that the Duke and Duchess of York and Cornwall returned from their 1901 tour of Australia bearing a collection of fairy tale books for their children.

Of course, although some of these fairies are favorably disposed to mortals, others like to harass, drown, or eat people. We've already discussed the British fey, so let's meet some of Australia's Aboriginal spirits now.

THE MIMI

Aboriginal myth says the mimi were once human and taught the original people how to hunt and paint. Now portrayed as tall, thin, usually benevolent fairies, they make their home in the rocks of Northern Australia.

THE RAINBOW SERPENT

A creator-destroyer spirit, this colorful, snakelike being supposedly birthed the earth and all its creatures. The Rainbow Serpent inhabits the lakes, rivers, and other waters of Australia and protects the land and the people. Rock paintings dating from 6,000 years ago depict this powerful spirit as a force in human life.

THE BUNJIL

Another creator spirit, Bunjil assumes the form of an eagle and his son spans the sky as the rainbow. Aboriginal folktales say he formed the earth and taught humans how to live together. He's now reputed to reside in the Black Range Scenic Reserve, in Victoria, a popular site known for its rock art.

THE BUNYIP

An evil spirit that occupies rivers, swamps, and waterholes, the bunyip may be a shapeshifter, for people describe it as looking like a starfish, having flippers, a horsetail, tusks, and/or fur. Some researchers think it might once have actually existed as a type of animal, now extinct.

THE MOKOTITI

According to the folklore of New Zealand's Maori people, this evil lizard spirit causes lung diseases and pulmonary birth defects. You'll also find mention of this being in Polynesian legends.

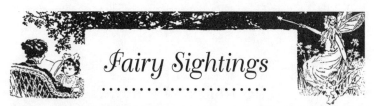

Fairy Sightings

In 1991, when Stephen Wagner was six years old, his family traveled to Calatagan Batangas, Philippines, for a vacation. One afternoon, after playing with friends, Stephen found himself standing near a garbage pit where he spotted a small, lifeless figure lying among the debris, and he assumed it was a cast-off toy. But as he continued studying it, he realized he was looking at the body of a male being with wings and a vivid, bruise-like wound on its chest. He knew immediately that the creature was dead and that it wasn't human. Stephen wanted to give the fairy a decent burial and felt guilty that he didn't have the opportunity to do so. He never forgot the strange, winged creature, and from that time on he never doubted that fairies exist.

FernGully's Fairies

Fairies have always been tree-huggers who protect the environment, and they still are. In the animated film *FernGully: The Last Rainforest* (1992), loggers threaten to destroy an Australian rainforest called FernGully and the fairies who live there. These innocent spirits have never encountered humans before, but they soon realize the danger mortals pose to them and their homeland. The story's heroine, Crysta, a cute, curious nature fairy with black hair and big green eyes, meets one of the lumberjacks named Zak and brings him down to size, literally. Once he can see the rainforest from the fairies' perspective, he comes to appreciate its beauty and joins the fairies to try to save it.

The film's villain, an oily, polluting bad guy named Hexxus (who makes viewers think of Exxon), was once a tree himself as the result of a spell cast on him for wreaking havoc in FernGully. Now the vengeful Hexxus is hell-bent on chopping down trees with a powerful machine called the Leveler. Eventually, the fairies succeed in trapping Hexxus in a tree once again, and the rainforest is safe, at least for now.

Australia's TV Fairies

From 2005–2009, Australian viewers sat glued to their televisions, under the spell of *The Fairies*. Totally silly, totally fun, the TV series featured two pretty girl fairies named Harmony and Rhapsody who lived in an enchanting garden along with a bee, a wizard, and a cake-baking elf. Combining human actors with animated characters, the fairies danced, sang, and fluttered about sprinkling fairy dust wherever they went. The show became an international success, and can still be seen on DVD.

Fairies in modern-day Asia and Australia have morphed from their ancient, mysterious, and often dangerous roots into pretty playmates that delight instead of frighten us. For instance, at Nickelodeon's Asian website, *www.nick-asia.com*, fairy fans can do fairy makeovers, play dress-up with the fairies, even adopt a fairy pet. By combining traditional mythology with contemporary fantasy, a rich and colorful tapestry of fairy lore has emerged.

"If you want your children to be intelligent, read them fairy tales. If you want them to be more intelligent, read them more fairy tales."

—Albert Einstein

ʃairies of the Americas

n an article for *Forbes* magazine, Todd Wilms proposed that our growing enthusiasm for fairies is directly linked to our increasing use of social media. The more we become engrossed in media and technology, he says, the more fragmented our lives become and the less genuine connection we engage in with other humans. Storytelling has always brought people together—around campfires or in sewing circles—while simultaneously taking us out of our ordinary reality into the realm of fantasy. Fairy tales also let us reconnect with the past and share familiar territory with one another. As we've already seen in earlier chapters of this book, fairy tales from around the world contain common themes and elements. "These common stories—myths, fairy tales, fantasy—all have those connective elements and bring us together in a very human way," explains Wilms. That's why fairy tales continue to delight us today, just as they have for centuries.

Disney's Fairies

You can't think of fairies without thinking of Disney. More than anyone in the world, Walt Disney and the company he founded have formed our contemporary conception of fairy folk and fairy tales. Begun in 1923 as The Disney Brothers Studio, the company won its first Academy Award nine years later with its first full-color animated film, *Flowers and Trees*, featuring talking plants that might have been enlivened by nature fairies. In 1937, Disney launched its first feature-length animated fairy tale film, *Snow White and the Seven Dwarfs*, and in 1955 Disneyland opened its doors to fantasy fans of all ages. Today, the Disney empire, which earned $5.7 billion in 2012, circles the globe and engages in virtually every form of family entertainment.

Although scores of fairies in Disney films have charmed audiences for decades, the most famous of all is Tinker Bell. This feisty little pixie, first introduced by J.M. Barrie in his 1904 play *Peter Pan*, made her screen debut in 1953. Since then, the Disney Company has chosen her as its mascot and even given her her own franchise: Disney Fairies. Her image is synonymous with Disney theme parks and she has her own direct-to-DVD film series. In 2010, Tink's personal star joined those of Hollywood's illuminati in the Walk of Fame.

Flitting about in her green mini-dress made of leaves, waving her magic wand, and scattering glittering pixie dust wherever she goes, Tinker Bell has transformed the way the world thinks about fairies and become the preeminent image of fey folk internationally. Not bad for a girl who started out as a mere spot of light reflected by a hand-held mirror.

Tinker Bell Trivia

. . . .

Q: How did Tinker Bell get her name?

A: She worked as a tinker (someone who mends pots, pans, and other household items) and in her early theatrical appearances a stagehand rang a bell to represent her voice.

Q: Where did Tinker Bell's creator believe fairies came from?

A: A baby's first laugh

Q: Who first played Tinker Bell in the movies?

A: Virginia Brown Faire in 1924

Q: What real-life woman served as the model for Disney's Tinker Bell (1953)?

A: Actress Margaret Kerry

Q: Where does Tinker Bell live?

A: Tinker's Nook

Q: In what kind of abode?

A: A teapot

We're Not in Kansas Anymore

It might be impossible to have been born in the United States during the last half of the twentieth century and *not* be familiar with the captivating musical film, *The Wizard of Oz* (1939), adapted from L. Frank Baum's fantasy novel *The Wonderful Wizard of Oz* (1900). Baum wrote thirteen sequels to his best-known book, including *Ozma of Oz* (1907), which featured an ageless and beautiful princess named Ozma who came from "a long line of fairy queens." Although it's not revealed in the first tale, it turns out that fairies created Oz as a magical kingdom full of otherworldly beings.

ENTERING FAIRYLAND

Water—an ancient symbol of mystery, imagination, and the unconscious—serves as a metaphor in *Ozma of Oz*. This powerful force transports protagonist Dorothy Gale into the magical Land of Ev, after she's swept overboard during a sea voyage. Clever Dorothy quickly realizes she's in fairyland because she sees lunchboxes instead of fruit hanging from trees. Soon she meets fanciful folks called "the Wheelers" who have wheels instead of hands and feet, and a clockwork character called Tik-Tok, reminiscent of the Tin Man. Ev's resident princess, Langwidere, orders Dorothy locked up in a tower, as threatened rulers are wont to do, although with the aid of a good witch and a magic carpet Dorothy manages to escape.

Finally, after many ups and downs, the story ends well, while leaving readers with the tantalizing possibility of yet another sequel. Ev's royal family—whom a usurping king turned into decorations for his palace—are restored to their rightful position, and the fairy Ozma uses magic to send Dorothy on to her original destination: Australia.

A MIRROR OF THE TIMES

The lovely Ozma reflects the Victorian era's changing images of fairies, from the frightening, cruel, and diabolically evil spirits of the Middle Ages to beautiful beings who are both gracious and good. Ozma, a pacifist at heart, wouldn't even hurt her worst enemies. She's also a socialist who establishes practices in Oz that let all citizens benefit equally from the fairyland's resources.

Interestingly, the publication of *Ozma of Oz* coincided with the economic Panic of 1907. At that time, financier J.P. Morgan and other "robber barons" manipulated the banking industry, and a small number of hugely wealthy conglomerates controlled the country's monetary resources. When a crash occurred, citizens demanded banking reforms.

Another socio-political theme presented in *Ozma of Oz*'s plotline is the king's practice of turning women and children into ornaments to adorn his palace. This plot element may comment on the restricted role of women during the turn of the twentieth century. Ozma's freeing of the royal family might reference the beginnings of feminism in the United States.

> "I think, at a child's birth, if a mother could ask a fairy godmother to endow it with the most useful gift, that gift should be curiosity."
>
> —Eleanor Roosevelt

Toot-Toot and the *Dresden Files* Fairies

Readers can't help being enchanted by the pizza-loving pixie Toot-Toot from Jim Butcher's *Dresden Files* series. Initially a pretty typical-looking fairy by today's standards, Toot stands about six inches tall with a pale, humanlike form and shimmering wings. He does have one colorful feature, however: magenta hair. His clothes don't resemble traditional fairy garb either—he wears a hat made from a bottle cap and carries a pin and a pencil as weapons. Later he straps on a shield fashioned from a Pepto-Bismol bottle and dons Ken-doll boots. Toot helps Chicago wizard Harry Dresden in numerous ways, from protecting his home from pests to providing information about Wee Folk activities to saving Harry's life. Over time, through his association with Harry and by facing daunting challenges, Toot grows in physical size as well as in character.

Butcher also takes readers inside the Summer and Winter courts (based on the Seelie and Unseelie courts of Scottish mythology; see Chapter 6). Queen Mab, the principal power of the Winter Court, comes off as a much more malevolent and manipulative fairy than either Shelley or Shakespeare portrayed her. Titania, the pretty fey lady from Shakespeare's *A Midsummer Night's Dream*, serves as head queen of the Summer Court. These two courts, however, probably bear more resemblance to King Arthur's than those of the real fey. Although Toot demonstrates great loyalty to Harry, most of the other fairies don't care much for mortals and actually look down on such pitifully inferior creatures.

The combination of mythology and modern-day kitsch, such as the peat moss villain at a Wal-Mart garden center, makes Butcher's supernatural characters both colorful and fun. And Toot-Toot is the most delightful of the bunch.

Fairies of the Native People of North America

Long before Europeans settled in the Americas, bringing their fairy tales with them, the indigenous people told stories of fairies and other supernatural beings. Some of these entities were nature spirits, others more closely resembled elves or gnomes, and still others were viewed as ancestor-guardians. Like fairies elsewhere, both nice and nasty types show up in native legends and lore.

THE KACHINAS

The Hopi and other Pueblo Indians in what's now the south-western United States honor kachinas as ancestral spirits present in clouds, rain, the wind, and nature in general. These spirits also make their home in the mountains at the Four Corners; however, legend says that at certain times of the year the kachinas live among the people in their villages in order to provide guidance and assistance to humans. An important part of mythology, these beings serve as a link between mortals and the realm of the spirits. Hundreds of different, distinct kachinas exist—each village has its own kachina.

To show respect for the spirits and to solicit their help, the Pueblo people dress in traditional costumes and perform rit-uals with music and dancing. Beautiful kachina dolls, intended as teaching tools for parents to share sacred knowledge with children, are a highly prized form of Southwestern art.

CHEROKEE SPIRITS

Cherokee legends describe three different types of nature spirits. Malicious spirits called the rock people—apparently angry at mor-tals for settling in their territory—steal human children. The mis-chievous, but not mean-spirited, laurel people play pranks on mortals, such as tangling their fishing lines. The friendliest of the lot, the dog-wood people, care for people and help them with chores.

Another type of fairy, similar to elves and humanlike in appearance, lives underground in the mountains of North and South Carolina. Known as the nunnehi, they rarely let mortals see them, though they're reported to sometimes slip into human territory incognito. Legend says they feel sympathy for the Cherokee and the suffering they endured at the hand of the white man, so the spirits sometimes aid the people. Like the Cherokee themselves, the nunnehi enjoy drumming and dancing.

LITTLE PEOPLE

The Shoshone speak about little people called the nimerigar who live in caves high in the San Pedro Mountains of New Mexico. Legend says they defended their territory with bows and poisoned arrows. In the 1930s, a mummy only about a foot high was discovered there, which mystified researchers. Could it have been the body of a nimerigar warrior?

Crow stories mention another group of little people who make their home in Montana's Pryor Mountains. Known as the nirumbee, these benevolent beings are said to aid the Crow in times of need and keep them safe. The Choctaw of the American Southwest also believed in a race of little people called the kwanokasha, who stood only about a foot or two in height.

The Passamaquoddy in Maine tell of little people called nagum-wasuck and mekumwasuck, whom only the Passamaquoddy can see. According to legend, these ugly creatures stand about three feet tall and live in the secluded forests near the Canadian border. Some accounts say they have hairy faces and long, floppy ears; others describe them with wrinkled, greenish skin. If one comes to your door asking for food, by all means feed it if you don't want trouble.

NATURE SPIRITS

In the forests of the Northwest, a dangerous spirit known as the bokwus with a painted face occasionally shows up. He doesn't like mortals who trespass into his territory and pushes hunters and fishermen into rivers, where they inevitably drown. The bokwus then steals their souls.

The jogah play a variety of beneficial roles in Iroquois mythology. The gandayah, a type of fertility fairy, nourish the soil so plants can grow. The gahonga reside in the rocks and rivers and are said to throw stones around. The handsome ohdows live underground, where they police the destructive spirits who cause earthquakes. When those dangerous spirits try to come to the earth's surface and shake things up, the ohdows stop them.

Fairies of the Native People of Central and South America

Tricksters and shapeshifters are popular beings in the legends of many Central and South American cultures. Some of these supernatural characters seem merely mischievous, but others can make human blood run cold. Although they may protect animals and treat them kindly, these spirits rarely show much consideration for mortals.

THE MAYAN ALUX

According to Mayan legends, spirits called aluxes occupy the jungles of the Yucatan Peninsula. The Mayans believe these fairies are the spirits of their ancestors as well as of the land itself—similar to nature fairies in other cultures. Only a few feet tall, these dwarf-like beings bear similarities to the Irish leprechauns.

The mischievous alux loves to play pranks on humans and may either scare mortals or protect them, depending on his mood and how you treat him. Be nice to him and he'll watch over your home and family; behave inconsiderately and he'll plague you with bad luck. One story says that a farmer should build a house on his land for the resident alux to live in for seven years. During this time, the alux will enhance crop growth, scare off predators and thieves, and call up the nurturing rains. When the seven-year period has ended, the farmer must seal up the house, imprisoning the alux inside to prevent him from rampaging through the countryside.

THE SIGUANABA OR CEGUA

If you approach this trickster spirit from behind, you might think she's a beautiful young woman with long, flowing hair wearing a diaphanous gown or nothing at all. But be wary, guys, if you decide to follow her down a lonely path in Central America at night—for when she turns around, the sight of her bony, horse-shaped skull can scare you senseless. Some legends say she has hooves instead of hands. She's also known to lead men—especially drunks and cheating husbands—into the wilderness, where they end up wandering lost and helpless forever.

THE CHULLACHAQUI

It's easy enough to get lost in the Amazon rainforest, but if you meet up with a chullachaqui you may never find your way back home again. Brazilian folklore describes this nature spirit as a gnome-like creature, ugly, bent, and greenish-brown in color. He protects the jungle and, in particular, the chullachaqui caspi tree said to provide medicinal benefits for everything from cuts to arthritis. Of course, to get to this wondrous tree you have to dodge the demon, which may not be worth the risk. How can you recognize him if you see him? One leg is shorter than the other, and a foot turns around backward.

THE CURURIPUR

Another unfriendly South American spirit who wears his feet backwards, the cururipur protects the forests and its creatures. He has a special fondness for turtles and tortoises. If a mortal hunts or harms his reptilian friends, this fiend leads the person into the forest, then ties him and tortures him to death.

THE POMBERO

Found in the forests of Paraguay and Argentina, the pombero looks sort of like early, cave-dwelling humans with long arms, stumpy legs, and lots of body hair. By all reports, he's both ugly and unpleasant. Legends say he comes out at night to torment mortals by stealing food, setting livestock loose, and trashing homes. In fact, this annoying guy gets blamed for just about anything that goes wrong—lost objects, flat tires, a bad day at work. At worst, he's rumored to force his attentions on women and can even impregnate them by simply touching them with his hand. Want to avoid this creep? Leave out gifts for him at night—he's partial to cigars and rum.

THE DUENDE

Said to live in the walls of houses, this small, sprite-like being who migrated to the New World from the Iberian Peninsula may either help or hinder humans. Some stories say the duende show lost people the way home. Others claim they lure mortals into the forests with their magical whistling. Young people especially should steer clear of this fairy, for he's reputed to cut off kids' toes and even eat children if he gets a chance. In modern-day parlance, the word also refers to a person with charisma.

THE ENCANTADO

Water fairies who can shapeshift into snakes, dolphins, or humans, Brazil's encantado share some characteristics with mermaids and other water spirits—they have musical talent, they're incredibly sexy, they stir up storms at sea, and they sometimes mate with mortals. And they love to party. Folklore warns people not to swim at night, for the encantado might capture them and whisk them away to an underwater realm known as Encante.

THE NAGUAL

A shapeshifting spirit who may appear as an animal or bird, the mysterious nagual can use its power to help or harm people. However, some sources describe the nagual as a shamanic being who can move easily between the various realms of existence, sometimes as an animal, sometimes as a human. The term also refers to a human sorcerer with magical powers that free him or her from the ordinary limitations of earth.

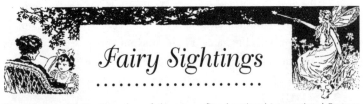

Fairy Sightings

Kim Del Rio, a lifetime member of the nonprofit educational International Fortean Organization (INFO) that researches unexplained phenomena, says she saw two fairies sitting on her bedroom windowsill. According to Del Rio, the yellow-green creatures, less than a foot high, had long arms and legs, thin torsos, and large eyes. They wore green garments, pointed shoes, and floppy, pointed hats. "Everything about them was subtle, no real sharp defined edges or colors," she posted on *www.paranormal .about.com* in 2003. "They were laughing at me, bending over with their hands on their knees, and pointing."

Holly Black's Modern Faerie Tales

If you think fairies are a thing of the past, author Holly Black would beg to differ with you. Her bestselling novels in the *Modern Faerie Tales* series—*Tithe* (2004), *Valiant* (2006), and *Ironside* (2008)—as well as some of her other books show fairy fans of all ages that, yes indeed, magic is still afoot today, even in some unlikely places.

In *Tithe*, sixteen-year-old Kaye Fierch isn't just the weird and independent daughter of a wannabe rock musician from New Jersey, she's also a fairy changeling with a bunch of fey friends. During the course of this modern-day fairy tale, she finds herself embroiled in a conflict between the ancient Seelie and the Unseelie fairy courts. As Kaye learns the hard way, fairies aren't all adorable little Tinks—they can be dangerous.

Valiant, the second in the series, tells the story of a seventeen-year-old runaway girl named Val who falls in love with a troll. While living in the subways of New York, she discovers that fairies really do exist—she even gets into using one of their drugs. The third book, *Ironside*, brings readers back to Kaye the changeling and the fairies of the Seelie and Unseelie courts. Kaye isn't safe among either group, especially at the hands of the scheming fairy queen Silarial. Once again, author Black exposes readers to the dark and deadly realms of the fey, in sharp contrast to the pretty pictures painted by some contemporary writers and filmmakers.

It seems people either love or hate the *Modern Faerie Tales* series. These aren't the sort of characters most parents want their teenagers to hang out with—they swear a lot, drink and do drugs, engage in casual sex, and don't play nice together. Fans of Black's books, however, praise their gritty realism and the alluring scenes in the fairy realm. Her tales remind us that the spirits of old were more likely to engage in murder and mayhem than to make wishes come true.

The Spiderwick Chronicles

Beginning in 2003, artist Tony DiTerlizzi and author Holly Black began publication of a series of lavishly illustrated stories and guides collectively called *The Spiderwick Chronicles*. When three children move into a dilapidated estate in Maine, they discover quickly that they are living on the edge of a fantastic and often dangerous world of fairies.

They find a curious book, *Arthur Spiderwick's Field Guide to the Fantastical World Around You*, which details the fairyland that exists within the estate and all around unseeing and unknowing mortals. Throughout the subsequent four books, the children—occasionally aided by creatures that include brownies, hobgoblins, and phookas—discover the secret behind the *Field Guide* and Arthur Spiderwick. They encounter the terrible ogre Mulgarath, Spiderwick's mortal enemy, and eventually succeed in vanquishing him.

Three subsequent books, *Beyond the Spiderwick Chronicles*, feature another group of children who encounter the world detailed in *The Spiderwick Chronicles* and must fight great dangers to stay alive.

Though DiTerlizzi and Black have indicated they would like to continue the stories, other projects have claimed their time. A feature film, *The Spiderwick Chronicles*, starring Freddie Highmore, was released in 2008.

Fairy Tales for Twenty-Somethings

Writer/illustrator Tim Manley updates many of our favorite fairy tales and gives them a humorous, modern twist in his colorful book *Alice in Tumblr-land: And Other Fairy Tales for a New Generation* (2013). Want to know how the familiar characters you heard about as a child turned out? Well, according to Manley, "The Ugly Duckling still feels gross compared to everyone else, but now she's got Instagram, and there's this one filter that makes her look awesome. Cinderella swaps her glass slippers for Crocs. The Tortoise and the Hare Facebook stalk each other. Goldilocks goes gluten-free. And Peter Pan finally has to grow up and get a job, or at least start paying rent."

The Tooth Fairy

The American custom of giving money to children when they first lose teeth comes from Europe. This ancient tradition is even mentioned in the *Eddas*, Northern Europe's mythological accounts that date back to the thirteenth century. In the United States today, according to a study done by Visa Inc. in 2013, a child who places a tooth beneath his or her pillow at night can expect to receive, on average, a gift from the Tooth Fairy in the amount of $3.70.

Obviously, fairies and fairy tales are here to stay, at least in the foreseeable future. From the early tales of the indigenous peoples of the Americas to the graphic novels and amazing animated films of today, fairy folk and other supernatural beings continue to awe, frighten, and charm us. Like their predecessors, contemporary stories teach us about good and evil, courage, loyalty, hope, self-acceptance, and transformation. They also make us laugh.

The Hidden Meanings of Fairies

"If you see the magic in a fairy tale, you can face the future."

—Danielle Steel

uring our whirlwind tour of fairies from around the world, we've covered a lot of ground, and yet we've barely scratched the surface. Fairies have captured the imagination of humans for so long, in so many ways, that no single book can even begin to tell their story. By revisiting old legends and myths from many lands, however, we've come to a better understanding of fairies and our relationship with them, and perhaps developed more respect for these magical beings.

Thanks to Tinker Bell and her friends, we no longer fear the fairies—we eagerly invite them into our lives to sing, dance, and laugh with us. Today, imaginative writers, artists, and cinematographers are expanding upon the rich body of fairy lore passed down to us through the centuries. Fairy tales, and legends in general, continue to evolve—they have to, for they are a part of us. As they evolve, they reflect societal trends as well as cultural, political, and spiritual ideas. They continue to teach us things we need to know, about ourselves and our world—and perhaps even the worlds beyond.

Guardians of the Earth

One thing we've learned about fairies is that they take their job as nature's guardians very seriously. When mortals injure plants or animals, the fairies swing into action, afflicting the offenders with disease or even death. In earlier times, things were easier for the ecology-minded fey—they only had to watch out for woodcutters and hunters. Of course, when humans believed that spirits dwelt in everything—plants and rocks, wind and water, thunder and lightning—the fairies had less trouble keeping mortals in line.

It may be no coincidence that as industry developed in the West during the Victorian era, people's interest in fairies grew as well. During that period the Brothers Grimm, Hans Christian Andersen, and Andrew Lang collected some of our favorite fairy tales, and enthusiastic audiences received them with acclaim. The concept of elementals—spirits that supposedly inhabit earth, air, fire, and water—also arose during the late nineteenth century among the Theosophists, Spiritualists, and other metaphysical groups.

Fairy tales had previously gained popularity in French society during the so-called Age of Enlightenment (1700–1800), as science and machinery moved to the fore. During the current digital age, we're witnessing yet another wave of fairy mania. It seems that when humans distance themselves from nature and from a mystical view of the universe, the fairies show up to remind us what's important and to keep us sane.

Today, the fey have their work cut out for them, fighting multinational corporations, insensitive politicians, and the onslaught of overpopulation. Never before have mortals possessed the power to unleash such widespread destruction on Planet Earth. Not only that, the fairies must deal with the ignorance of humans who either misunderstand the fey or doubt their existence altogether.

Perhaps that's why we're experiencing a resurgence of fairy fascination in the twenty-first century. We need the fairies to sprinkle our lives with light, joy, and pretty pixie dust, and to restore our faith in infinite possibilities. We need the fairies to show us how to live in harmony with nature, and to help us reconnect to our spirituality in a technology-driven world.

Fairies Are Not What They Seem

Myths and legends often depict fairies as shapeshifters and tricksters. Humans beware! The fey are not what they seem to be, and quite frankly you can't trust them. That cute little pixie no larger than your hand might steal your kids as soon as you turn your back. That bodacious blonde might want your body, but not in the way you imagine.

When you're dealing with fairies, keep in mind that everything you think you know is wrong. The fey just don't see things the way we do, and the rules of their realm differ dramatically from ours. Human limitations don't apply to them. For instance, they can cast spells known as glamours that enable them to appear in whatever form they choose. They may show themselves as animals, birds, insects, humans, hybrid creatures—whatever suits their purposes. Furthermore, they slip in and out of the realms of earth and Faerie at will, and if you foolishly go along with them you'll wind up completely confused.

Deception rears its head every day in our contemporary human world, too, not just in fairyland. News manipulation. Advertising. "Reality" TV. Photoshopped images. Cosmetic surgery. Special effects. The line between fact and fantasy grows increasingly thin. But media aside, we all engage in a subtle type of illusion. We all have outer personas that mask our inner natures. As eleven-year-old Lettie, in Neil Gaiman's *Ocean at the End of the Lane*, replies when asked what the monster Ursula Monkton really is, "Nobody actually looks like what they really are on the inside. You don't. I don't. People are much more complicated than that."

Fairies, therefore, may represent the shapeshifter element in each of us. Without judgment or criticism, the fey ask us to assess how we present ourselves to other people and what we hope to gain from the illusion. What different roles do we take on— parents, lovers, children, employees/ employers, citizens in our communities? Are we pretending to be something more than what we are? Are we putting up a false front in order to win the guy, the job, the approval of friends, family, or colleagues? What are we willing to do to achieve our ends? And how have we deluded ourselves in the process?

> "Fairy tales were not my escape from reality as a child; rather, they were my reality—for mine was a world in which good and evil were not abstract concepts, and like fairy-tale heroines, no magic would save me unless I had the wit and heart and courage to use it widely."
>
>  —Terri Windling

Dual Natures

Some fairies are nice guys, some are miserable creeps—just like humans. Scottish mythology even divides fairies into opposing camps according to their temperaments and behavior: the Seelie (light/benevolent) and the Unseelie (dark/malevolent) courts. But as we've seen already, even the friendly fey are capricious creatures who can turn on you in a heartbeat for no apparent reason.

The dual natures of fairies may represent the two forces of good and evil in the world. The mythologies and religions of all cultures speak of these polarities—it seems that we can't have one without the other. Jungian psychology explores the duality of our individual natures: the outer, conscious side and the inner, unacknowledged or "shadow" side. Most of us fear or loathe the shadow part—whether or not we're aware of it—and may project it onto other people, seeing in them what we deny or dislike in ourselves. The French refer to the shadow as *la bête noire*, the black beast, and it's a central theme in many fairy tales. Remember Gabrielle-Suzanne Barbot de Villeneuve's story "La Belle et la Bête" (Beauty and the Beast)? Belle must befriend the beast before it can transform—and so must we.

Fairy Sightings

In his book *The Coming of the Fairies*, Sir Arthur Conan Doyle, who wrote the Sherlock Holmes series, cited Charles W. Leadbeater's varied descriptions and experiences with fairies. "In England the emerald-green kind is probably the commonest, and I have seen it also in the woods of France and Belgium, in far-away Massachusetts, and on the banks of the Niagara river. The vast plains of the Dakotas are inhabited by a black-and-white kind which I have not seen elsewhere, and California rejoices in a lovely white-and-gold species which also appears to be unique."

Lost in Fairyland

One of the most common tricks fairies around the world play on humans is leading us deep into the woods, or into some other strange and indecipherable world, where we lose sight of all that's familiar to us and wander dazed and confused for an indeterminable period of time—perhaps forever. In fairy tales, the forest serves as a metaphor for the unknown. We dread going there, but ultimately we must plunge onward—guided, as it were, by magical beings—if we are to unravel the age-old mysteries and grow into our full potential. The forest also represents the unconscious, where all fears, memories, and wisdom lie, the quintessential realm of darkness waiting to be illuminated and explored. It symbolizes the "road less traveled," the primal, unadulterated, and uncharted path that leads us away from conventional, "safe" thinking and into the uncertain and creative territory of our own psyches.

Getting lost in fairyland can be one of the most enlightening things that could ever happen to a mortal. Following the fey into the forest represents reconnecting with what you know to be true in your heart of hearts, rather than going along with what society has taught you to believe. It signifies relying on your intuition, not just your intellect. And, as so many legends warn, you may never come back—for once you've gone beyond the limits of mundane thinking, plumbed your depths, and achieved a heightened sense of awareness, you can never return to the ordinary world you inhabited before the fairies intervened.

Immortality in the Realm of the Fey

Old age, sickness, and death haunt humans—we can't shake the specter lurking just around the corner, reminding us of what's in store for us. Wouldn't it be nice to be a fairy and live for hundreds or thousands of years, without losing your looks or vitality? To dwell in a timeless realm where the hardships, blinkered vision, and physical limitations of earth don't exist? Of course we envy the fey.

Legends and myths about fairies predate Christianity, Islam, and some of the other religions of today's world. Early myths link fairies with ancient deities or consider fairies to be minor divinities. The Irish sidhe, the Greek nymphs, and the Indian nagas, for example, supposedly descended from gods and goddesses. Other legends suggest that mortals evolved from fairies, and many tales speak of human-fairy relationships as well as their blended offspring, suggesting that we all have otherworldly connections.

Another recurring theme in fairy tales is that people leave Planet Earth and disappear into the glorious realm of Faerie, where they become immortal and forget about the material world they left behind. In many aspects, fairyland sounds a lot like heaven—a wondrous place from which we came and to which we can return, if we relinquish our attachment to the earth. Our ancestors may have cobbled their religious ideas and conceptions about an afterlife onto Faerie, or vice versa, which might help to explain our profound and unrelenting attraction to fairies.

Fairies Forever

In days of old, people everywhere believed in all sorts of supernatural beings, including fairies. Today, most scientific and rational folks give fairies little credence. But the fact that we can't prove fairies exist doesn't mean they don't. William Faulkner once said, "Facts and truth really don't have much to do with each other." Once upon a time, the world of bacteria would have seemed mysterious and fantastic. And just because people didn't know about Pluto until the twentieth century doesn't mean it wasn't out there.

Science seeks to explain everything—but maybe we don't want everything explained. We don't want all the magic to go out of life. We want to remain connected to the secret parts of our inner beings, to the ancient mysteries, and to the most distant outposts of the universe. We want to believe. And as long as we do, the fairies will remain.

"Faeries, come take me out of this dull world,
For I would ride with you upon the wind,
Run on the top of the dishevelled tide,
And dance upon the mountains like a flame."

—William Butler Yeats, *The Land of Heart's Desire*

Bibliography

Alexander, Skye. *Mermaids: The Myths, Legends, & Lore*. (Avon, Mass.: F+W Media, Inc., 2012).

_____. *The Secret Power of Spirit Animals*. (Avon, Mass.: F+W Media, Inc., 2013).

Andersen, Hans Christian, Haviland, Virginia, and Haugaard, Erik Christian. *Hans Christian Andersen: The Complete Fairy Tales and Stories*. (New York: Anchor Books, 1983).

Armstrong, Karen. *A Short History of Myth*. (Edinburgh: Canongate U.S., 2006).

Ashliman, D.L. *A Guide to Folktales in the English Language*. (New York: Greenwood Press, 1987).

Barrie, J.M. *Peter Pan; or, the Boy Who Wouldn't Grow Up*, first performed 1904.

_____. *Peter and Wendy*. (Boston: IndyPublish.com, original copyright 1911).

Baum, L. Frank. *Ozma of Oz*. (Chicago: Reilly and Barton, 1907).

_____. *The Wonderful Wizard of Oz*. (New York: Signet Classics, 1984).

Bennett, William J. (ed.). *The Children's Book of Virtues*. (New York: Simon and Schuster, 1995).

Bettelheim, Bruno. *Uses of Enchantment: The Meaning and Importance of Fairy Tales*. (New York: Vintage Books, 2010).

Black, Holly. *Tithe*. (New York: Simon Pulse, 2004).

_____. *Valiant*. (New York: Margaret K. MacElderry Books, 2006).

_____. *Ironside*. (New York: Margaret K. MacElderry Books, 2007).

Blair, Nancy. *Goddesses for Every Season*. (Rockport, Mass.: Element Books, 1995).

Blavatsky, Madame Helena. *Isis Unveiled*. (Wheaton, Ill.: Quest Books, 1997).

Bord, Janet. *Fairies: Real Encounters with Little People*. (New York: Bantam Doubleday Dell Publishing Group, 1997).

Bow, Erin. *Plain Kate*. (New York: Arthur A. Levine Books, 2010).

Bradley, Marion Zimmer. *The Mists of Avalon*. (New York: Ballantine Publishing Group, 1982).

Briggs, Katharine Mary. *An Encyclopedia of Fairies* (New York: Pantheon Books, 1976).

Chaucer, Geoffrey. *The Canterbury Tales*. (Project Gutenberg, *www.gutenberg.org*).

Clarke, Susanna. *Jonathan Strange and Mr. Norrell*. (New York: Bloomsbury Publishing, 2004).

Colfer, Eoin and Donkin, Andrew. *Artemis Fowl: The Arctic Incident*. (New York: Hyperion Books, 2009).

Cunningham, Allan. *The Lives of the Most Eminent British Painters, Sculptors, and Architects*. (London: J. Murray, 1830, *http://archive.org*).

Dennys, Nicholas Belfield, PhD. *The Folk-Lore of China*. (London: Trubner and Co., 1876).

Doorly, Moyra. "Fairy Types, Dos and Don'ts, Iceland and Fairy Forests." (*www.forteantimes .com/features/articles/173/fairy_types_dos_and_donts_iceland_and_fairy_forests.html*).

_____. "Invitation to Elfland." (*www.forteantimes.com/features/articles/172/invitation_to_ elfland.html*).

Doyle, Sir Arthur Conan. *The Coming of the Fairies*. (Charleston, S.C.: BiblioBazaar, 2008, original copyright 1922).

Dubois, Pierre. *The Complete Encyclopedia of Elves, Goblins, and Other Little Creatures*. (New York: Abbeville Press, 2005).

Encyclopedia Britannica (*www.brittanica.com*).

Evans Wentz, W.Y. *The Fairy-Faith in Celtic Countries*. (London: Oxford University Press, 1911).

Gaiman, Neil. *Fragile Things*. (New York: HarperCollins, 2006).

_____. *The Ocean at the End of the Lane*. (New York: HarperCollins, 2013).

Gilbert, W.S. and Sullivan, Arthur. *Iolanthe*. (First produced in London, 1882).

Glancey, Jonathan. *Nagaland: A Journey to India's Forgotten Frontier* (London: Faber and Faber, Ltd., 2011).

Grimm, Jacob and Grimm, Wilhelm. *Children's and Household Tales*. (Project Gutenberg, *www.gutenberg.org*, originally published 1812).

Hills, Suzannah. "Sleeping beauties," *The Daily Mail—MailOnline*, August 9, 2013 (*www .dailymail.co.uk*).

Ingpen, Robert and Page, Michael. *Encyclopedia of Things That Never Were*. (New York: Penguin, 1998).

Japanese American National Museum (*www.janmstore.com*).

Keightley, Thomas. *The Fairy Mythology: Illustrative of the Romance and Superstition of Various Countries*. (London: George Bell & Sons, 1892).

Kready, Laura Fry. *A Study of Fairy Tales*. (Project Gutenberg, *www.gutenberg.org*).

Lagerlöf, Selma. *The Changeling*. (New York: Knopf Books, 1992).

Lang, Andrew. *The Arabian Nights*. (Project Gutenberg, *www.gutenberg.org*).

MacDonald, Margaret Read. *The Storyteller's Sourcebook*. (Detroit, Mich.: Neal-Schuman Publishers, Inc., 1982).

Manley, Tim. *Alice in Tumblr-land: And Other Fairy Tales for a New Generation*. (New York: Penguin Books, 2013).

Oregon University Libraries. (*http://library.uoregon.edu*).

Perrault, Charles. *Stories or Tales from Times Past, with Morals, or Tales of Mother Goose*. (*www.pitt.edu*, posted by D.L. Ashliman, 1998–2013, originally published 1697).

Ramanujan, A.K. *Folktales from India*. (New York: Pantheon Books, 1991).

Shakespeare, William. *A Midsummer Night's Dream*.

Shelley, Percy Bysshe. *Queen Mab*. (South Australia: University of Adelaide Library, *http://ebooks.adelaide.edu.au*).

Spenser, Edmund. *The Faerie Queene.* (Project Gutenberg, *www.gutenberg.org,* originally published in 1590).

Time-Life Books (eds.). *The Enchanted World: Fairies and Elves.* (Alexandria, Va.: Time-Life Books, Inc., 1984).

Tolkien, J.R.R. *The Hobbit.* (Sydney: George Allen & Unwin Ltd., 1937).

Toney, Veronica. "Why Haven't We Outgrown Fairy Tales?" *The Washington Post,* June 25, 2013.

Twain, Mark. *Joan of Arc.* (San Francisco: Ignatius Press, 1989).

Wilms, Todd. "SAPVoice: The Unequivocal Connection Between Social Media and Myths, Fairy Tales, & Fantasy," *Forbes,* June 5, 2012 (*www.forbes.com*).

Wilson, G. Willow. *Alif, the Unseen.* (New York: Grove Press, 2012).

Yeats, William Butler. *Fairy and Folk Tales of Ireland.* (New York: Touchstone, 1973.)

Yolen, Jane and Stemple, Heidi. *Fairy Tale Feasts.* (Northampton, Mass.: Interlink Publishing Group, 2006).

Zipes, Jack (ed.). *The Great Fairy Tale Tradition: From Straparola and Basile to the Brothers Grimm.* (New York: W.W. Norton and Co., 2000).

Online Resources

www.about.com

www.amazon.com

www.ancient-mythology.com

www.angelfire.com

www.australianmuseum.net.au

www.buzzymag.com

www.celtic-twilight.com

www.cultureofchinese.com

www.en.wikipedia.com

www.endicott-studio.com

www.fairies-secrets.com

www.fairycongress.com

www.fairysource.com

www.fairiesworld.com

http://fairies.zeluna.net

www.goodreads.com

www.multicoloreddiary.blogspot.com

www.mythicarts.com

www.mythologydictionary.com

www.nytimes.com

www.oldrussia.net

www.opusarchives.org

www.pantheon.org

www.paranormal.about.com

www.paranormalhaze.com

www.surlalunefairytales.blogspot.com

www.talesoffaerie.blogspot.com

www.theoi.com

www.timelessmyths.com

www.urban-fairies.com

www.viola.bz/sirin

www.warriorsofmyth.wikia.com

www.whats-your-sign.com

www.zeluna.net

Index

ABOUT THE AUTHOR

SKYE ALEXANDER is the award-winning author of more than thirty fiction and nonfiction books, including *Mermaids: The Myths, Legends, & Lore* and *The Secret Power of Spirit Animals*. Her stories have been published in anthologies internationally, and her work has been translated into a dozen languages. She divides her time between Texas and Massachusetts.